TELL ME YOU
Need Me

A SEARCH AND SEDUCE NOVEL

JOYA RYAN

Entangled Publishing, LLC
2614 South Timberline Road
Suite 109
Fort Collins, CO 80525
Visit our website at www.entangledpublishing.com.

Brazen is an imprint of Entangled Publishing, LLC. For more information on our titles, visit www.brazenbooks.com.

Edited by Stephen Morgan & Ava Jae
Cover design by Heather Howland
Cover art from iStock

Manufactured in the United States of America

First Edition November 2015

ENTANGLED
BRAZEN

To Brett

I'm so proud of you. You're a pain in the ass sometimes, but you're the best brother in the world and I love you like crazy. You always make me laugh and no matter what, I have your back. This may be a romance novel, but I dedicate it to you anyway because secretly, deep down, I know you read them. Love you, buddy!

Chapter One

G age McGraw took a pull from his beer then set the long bottle down on the bar. He spun the brown glass on the counter and watched the alcohol swish inside.

Christ, he was nervous. So nervous he was fucking fidgeting.

He was a New Yorker, so the small-town bar he was in shouldn't have affected him. He'd been in Beaufort, North Carolina a handful of times. It might not be large, but the area was built on a wide variety of outdoor activities. Between the ocean, forest, and vast terrain, tourists flocked to this haven of adventure yearly. Which, unfortunately, meant that every summer people braved the mountains and got lost.

That was where he came in as a lead member of the Search & Rescue team. He traveled the country a lot, usually on missions to track, find, and recover. It was what he did best; what he loved. After getting shrapnel in the leg and being honorably discharged from the military a few years ago, it was also the only job he could do that allowed him to use the skills the US government had taught him.

The local S&R team now taught a survival skills boot camp for anyone going into the mountains without a guide. Plenty of people still got lost, but at least this year the boot camps seemed to have done some good, because when Gage had arrived, there hadn't been any immediate S&Rs to perform. Instead, his boss said he'd be spending the next few weeks training new S&R recruits.

Which was where tonight's waiting game at the bar came in. A little free time meant he had a chance to focus on the thing he'd been obsessing over since an S&R last month had nearly cost him his life.

He'd been out searching for a lost climber in the mountains. He'd found him at the bottom of a cliff, his leg broken, the person barely hanging on. So Gage had put on his harness, climbed down the rocky wall, told the climber not to worry, he would be right there—

And the harness that'd been holding him over a fifty-foot drop had snapped. His fingernails dug hopelessly into the rock as he plummeted down the side of the damn mountain and dropped off into the open air, nothing to stop his fall but the hard ground far below.

It was stupid, dumb luck that his flailing hand had found the rope hanging above him.

It'd hit him then—the reality of his mortality. It'd never bothered him before; being injured or dying went hand in hand with rescuing people from dangerous situations. But this had been more. He didn't have anyone permanent in his life—who would his team have told if he hadn't walked away? Who would care? He didn't have a family or a girlfriend. If he'd died, no one would have missed him.

He was here to change that.

He'd come back into town and to this bar with a plan that would take longer than a weekend to carry out. Damn if he wasn't nervous, though. He could use a little stress relief.

Small town or not, Honey's was always busy. The restaurant and bar was where the whole town seemed to hang out. There was a sense of community here. With locals hovering around the pool tables, fried food, and good music, he couldn't help but imagine what it'd be like to set down some roots here. Have a place and a person to come home to.

"Vodka cranberry please," a sultry voice said to the bartender. Gage glanced to his left, where a tall blonde shimmied her way in and placed her hands on the counter.

The woman spared him a glance. Barely. But enough to catch a glimpse of the greenest eyes he'd ever seen. She tapped her fingers on the bar and leaned forward, waiting to be served.

She was lithe and lean, with curves in all the right places. Her short denim skirt barely covered her ass. Her tank top was simple and black. The thin straps would take little more than a tug of his finger to break. Two seconds was all he'd need to have those high, round breasts bared for his mouth—

"Never seen a woman before, city boy?" she asked.

Shit—he was staring. Gage hid his flush with a smile and recovered quickly.

"I've seen plenty of women." He grabbed his beer and faced her. "Which is why I know when to appreciate an exceptionally fine one."

That got her to look at him. He unleashed a grin he knew firsthand could melt panties, and he waited for her to swoon.

To her credit, she didn't.

She looked him over, those stern emeralds pausing on his chest, then lower. She might be playing coy now, but there was heat in her eyes. He felt it with every sweep of her gaze. And boom! There it was. The lip bite.

She tugged that plump bottom flesh between her teeth so quickly he almost missed it. She was definitely sizing him up right back. And judging by the way she wet her lips, she liked what she saw.

The bartender placed her drink in front of her.

"Put it on my tab," Gage said, and the bartender nodded.

"Dishing pretty compliments and buying me a drink won't get you what you're after," she said.

He drank his beer. With his feet on the floor, he opened his knees and relaxed back in his seat. When someone bumped into her and she shifted toward him, effectively planting her hips between his legs, he smiled.

"Really? How do you know what I'm after?"

She took a drink. The ice clinked in her glass, and he caught a whiff of tart cranberries. She was sweet and sour in all the best ways—he could fucking smell it. Now if he could just taste it…

"I'm a pretty good judge of people." She shrugged. "I can also read your mind."

"That right?" He slung one elbow on the back of his bar seat and moved his knee enough to brush along her outer thigh. "Well, I do already have you in a house. Surely there must be bedrooms around here."

The restaurant they were in had a unique layout. It was a massive old Victorian house turned into the local watering hole complete with bar, tables, and multiple rooms. There was even an indoor balcony. The second floor nestled right above them was meant for large parties, but it was currently closed off and dark.

"But we can talk more about bedtime later. By all means, don't leave me in suspense with your mind-reading skills," he finished.

Her green gaze slowly slid along his body; that sinful expression had his cock throbbing.

"You come across as casual, but you clearly like control." She tilted her head, examining him further. "You're strong. Hold a sense of command. You issue an order and expect it to be followed."

He clenched his fist to keep from reaching out to touch her. She was easily pegging down details about him few people knew.

"If I issued an order, would you follow it?" he countered.

She smiled. "Nope." She leaned in, and her mouth brushed his earlobe. "But you'd like that. You want a woman a little dirty, naughty, and able to take it rough."

"What makes you think I'm rough?" he rasped.

She glanced at his free hand, then his chest. "Because judging by the way you're holding your breath and grinding your teeth, you're barely holding back from tossing me on this bar and taking me right here." She shook her head slightly, letting the silky blond strands fall down her back. "I think you'd like a little fight in your woman."

Every muscle he had flexed. Ready to prove her right. "Clearly you'd have some fight in you."

She nodded. "I just don't know if you can handle it, city boy."

"Oh, I can bend you to my will."

"Prove it."

That shot his semihard cock to full attention. Her nearness was enough to make his whole body tense, ready to take her *now*. She was daring him to be rough with her, and she was right—he liked it hard. A little begging. A little pain. And a hell of a lot of pleasure.

The kind of power she wielded over him should drive him crazy, but it didn't. She was different than any woman he'd ever been with. She excited him easily and made herself a challenge. And damn, did he like every second of it.

She took another drink, and condensation from her glass dripped onto her cleavage. He licked his lips—God, how he wanted to catch that droplet with his tongue. But before he came up with another witty line, she finished her vodka, turned, and walked away without a word.

No fucking way was he letting her go.

Hot on her heels, he bounded after her. He followed her into the shadows, went around the back of the bar, and strode quickly until he finally found her edging into a shadowy corner.

"You're walking away from me, huh?" he said.

She opened a side door, arched an eyebrow at him over her shoulder, and climbed the stairs. He followed her up, and his heart pounded as they neared the closed-down balcony over the bar. Twenty-five feet below them, everyone enjoyed themselves, none the wiser that he was with a sexy woman in the dark above.

She moved to one of the booths hiding in the shadows, and he grabbed her arm and spun her to face him. A lusty hue lit up her eyes.

"You're chasing me?" she whispered.

He moved her against the wall, kicked her feet apart with his, and pressed his body against hers. The loud crowd from downstairs echoed around them, but he held her tight in the shadows. This was it. He was going to take her right there. And she was going to let him.

More, she was going to *like* it. He could see it in the way she licked her lips. She was as hungry for him as he was for her.

He scraped his jean-clad knee along the insides of her spread thighs. Even with the barrier of their clothes, her heat surrounded him.

"I've been chasing you for a while." He pushed her skirt up, grabbed the back of her thighs, and lifted her. She wrapped those long legs around him, and damn it felt good. Gage glanced down. She wasn't wearing panties. He smiled and whispered against her lips, "And it looks like you missed me too, Chloe."

"I have," she breathed. "But I like making you work for it."

Yeah, he liked working for it, too. These little games they played never got old. Whenever he was back in town, they pretended it was their first time. Though the stretch before they gave in to each other had dwindled down to minutes.

He couldn't wait any longer. He had her in his arms, and it was time he properly reacquainted himself with her body.

Chloe clutched Gage. Ever since their first encounter two years ago, her life had been one wild, sex-crazed weekend at a time.

The perfect thing about Gage was he was as allergic to commitment as she was. Their sporadic rendezvous a few times a year was the kind of setup she could handle. She could commit to her life, the town she loved, and the people in it. But a man? She'd seen what her mother went through with her father. She'd loved him until the day she died, even after he'd left both of them years ago.

Chloe had tried dating men once she'd gone out on her own, and they'd all shown her the same thing. None of them had any staying power—at least not for her.

No, never commit to a man. She'd never become so attached to someone that she'd pine for them long after they were gone. Which was why Gage was so perfect.

He was a one weekend at a time kind of guy, and they had clear expectations. Sure, he was the only man she'd been with since she met him two years ago, but it didn't mean anything. He was just so good at what he did to her that she didn't need anyone else until he came back around again. She would never wait for him.

He was back in town, and now it was time for a fix. Simple.

Gage was strong, confident, and sexy as sin. He took her over and made her feel more than passion, more than heat, more than anything she could explain. He let her be strong while making her beg. Never in all the blissful weekends they'd spent together did he take it easy on her. She loved his dark and rough side, and he delivered every time.

She needed another taste to last her until next time he blew into town. That was all.

"You dressed for me," he whispered against her mouth. "I like it." Truth was, normally she was a jeans and T-shirt kind of girl. But when Gage came around, she often spent an hour tearing through her closet thinking of the perfect outfit. But he didn't need to know that.

"I didn't dress up, just figured this was easy access. It's all about logistics, after all."

"Uh-huh." He grinned, gripped her thigh harder, and bit her neck. She wove her fingers into his hair and sighed as he nibbled on her skin.

"So it's all about the sex?" he asked.

She nodded. "Well, yeah."

He scoffed and ran his lips along her collarbone. She tugged tightly on his hair—he grabbed her arm in a flash and pinned it to her side.

"Getting wild already, sweetheart?" he growled against her breasts, then bit her tank top.

Her breath hitched in her throat. "Maybe." She scraped her heel against his ass like a spur. He pushed her harder into the wall and cupped her throat with his free hand.

This was what she wanted. The kind of fix only he could give. He took away her need for control and gave her the freedom to simply feel. Let her experience nothing but pleasure. All of her stress and sadness vanished for a night at a time whenever Gage was around. She got out her aggression—and he got her off in a way she'd never experienced with another.

"If I didn't know any better, I'd think you liked getting tossed around a bit." He gently squeezed her neck. Not enough to hurt, but the calluses on his palms scratched the sensitive column of her throat when she swallowed.

"You know I do," she said. "And you like giving it rough as much as I like taking it." She lifted her chin, looking deeply into the dark pools of his eyes. "Good line in there by the way," she said and crushed her mouth against his. He plunged his tongue inside and kissed her like he hadn't seen her in four months—which he hadn't. She loved the urgency and lust behind his every move.

"I meant every word," he said between heavy breaths. "You bit your lip and I thought I'd toss you on the counter and fuck you right there."

She moaned—God, how she wanted him to have her right now.

"You know what that does to me." He yanked down her tank top and latched onto a nipple. "I'll play your little games, but you took it too far. I could barely stay in my seat."

With both her hands free now, she grabbed his lower back and yanked him closer. His hips pushed against her thighs until the dull pain of forming bruises stung her skin. She wanted more. She loved the ache—the promise of wild still to come.

He held her tightly, but she moved however she could. Rocking against his hard-on, brushing her face against his stubble, running her hands through his hair, anything to get that zing of contact. It'd been so long since she felt him—she was about to explode. In a few seconds, she'd get off with little more than a skillfully placed grind.

"You show up, no panties, no bra, and you know what happens?" He sucked on her sensitive peak.

"I hope you fucking me happens, because I can't wait."

She spurred her heel against his ass again, begging for

more. Calling out the dominant side she loved so much. And he rose to the request.

"No waiting for you, sweetheart," he rasped. He yanked her off the wall and pressed her stomach-first onto the ground, facing the balcony ledge. Gage gathered her wrists and held them firmly against the small of her back.

She wiggled to test his strength—he was unbendable. Her tank top was pulled up to her neck, and the cold wood floor pressing against her bare breasts sent shivers down her spine. A cool draft hit the exposed cleft of her ass.

He had her pinned. Laid out flat and *pinned*.

"You see them all down there? How many of those people do you know?" he whispered in her ear.

She lifted the side of her face off the floor enough to glance down over the ledge. It was impossible to move much, but she wiggled anyway, daring him to tighten his hold. Like a boa constrictor delivering little pulses of strength as he slowly stole her struggle. Wetness flashed between her legs and sensitized her skin another degree.

Though she was mostly in the shadows, her head was in a strip of light. If someone were to look up, they'd see her face as she looked down at them. Would they see Gage's glowing dark eyes behind her? She could imagine the sight. Only her face hinted at what was being done to her body in the dark.

"Everyone," she whispered. "I know everyone in the bar."

And she did. Beaufort was a small town, and she'd grown up there. Her own mother had lived in this very house before she'd transformed it into a restaurant and bar. It was the only home Chloe had ever known. Where she and her mom had waited all those years for her dad to come back.

Chloe struggled harder, pushing the memories out of her mind. She just wanted to forget and feel.

"Little fiery tonight." He hiked her skirt up and held her firmly against the floor with her legs spread. "If one of those friends of yours looked up here, what do you think they'd see?"

With one hand still grabbing her wrists, the other palmed her ass hard. She gasped and smiled. Gage liked her mouth and spirit in more ways than one. It was time to test him. Challenge him.

"They'd probably see you taking your sweet-ass time fondling me instead of fucking me hard like you should—"

Slap—his hand came across her bare ass, and she moaned. This was what she wanted. The intense, rough man she got to scratch and claw at while he spanked back.

Gage chuckled. "You really want to push me tonight?"

"I'm starting to wonder if you've lost your touch, city boy."

He growled. She smiled at the clink of his belt loosening and the crackle of a ripping condom wrapper.

"Why don't you tell me if I've lost my touch?" He rubbed the head of his cock against her wet folds, teasing her, tempting her—and then he thrust deep inside.

She gasped and rocked forward. Her body flush against the ground and spread wide, he withdrew and then slammed back inside her.

"I don't hear you saying anything now, sweetheart. Lost your nerve? Or are you trying to be quiet so no one hears you moan for me and sees you getting fucked hard"—he pulled out and thrust again—"the way you like it."

"I do. So much," she whispered. She was completely immobile. Gage still had her wrists trapped with one hand, and he wrapped his free hand around her middle and lay completely on top of her. She was at his mercy and surrounded by his strength. And she loved it.

"I know." He pumped again, deeper, and she stifled a scream. He hit her perfectly, every damn time. "You're wet and I didn't even get my hands or tongue on this tight pussy."

He pistoned in and out, snaked his arm around her further, and locked his leg around hers.

She tilted her head back and leaned into him so she could run her teeth along his jaw. When he slammed into her again, she bit down.

"Fuck, baby," he moaned. His breath washed over her lips. "Do you know how many times I've thought of you?" He thrust harder. "Thought of being right here?" Faster.

If it was half the amount of times she'd thought of him, it was daily. Which was why she'd lured him out here instead of drawing the night out. She wanted him to take her like this, and she'd take advantage of every second she had with him for the twenty-four to forty-eight hours she was given.

"Tell me, Chloe, what have you thought of?" He wrapped her tighter in his arms, and she relaxed. Let him have her. She didn't have to do anything but lie there and take it. The fight would come and go. For now, she reveled in him taking her over.

She panted. "I've thought of you. Doing exactly this to me."

"Like this?" He surged inside again. Each ridge and curve of his cock stretched and slid so perfectly that every last nerve ending sparked like a flickering lightbulb.

"Yes," she moaned. Her sheath was tightening, so close to ecstasy. Her eyes fluttered open to see the bar patrons carrying on their conversations downstairs. They had no idea she was ready to come around the man who stole her thoughts every time he came into town.

"Do you touch yourself and think of me?"

"Yes…but it's never good enough. Deep enough…hard enough."

Gage groaned, like she'd said the exact right thing. He picked up the pace even more. She couldn't breathe around the pleasure.

"So you don't drench your own fingers like this?" He buried himself deep and stirred. "Because you're weeping for me, sweetheart."

"Only with you." He shifted his hips, hitting deeper than ever before—she gasped. "Gage…yes…right there."

A flash of white stole her vision, and red heat burst through her veins like a gunshot. It sparked and burned as it rushed from her core to her scalp, pricking and sizzling everything in between.

His hand covered her mouth as she screamed with her release. Her eyes widened—if his firm palm hadn't stifled her cries, she would have brought the roof down.

She panted and moaned against his hand, squeezing her eyes shut as her orgasm went on and on. Snapping her skin like angry, lusty fingers. Sharp, and loud, and heady. Gage was right there, ready to come with her.

He hardened another degree inside her, and the sensation kicked her already unrelenting passion into overdrive. She pressed her mouth further against his palm, trying to contain her yell. Gage bit down on the curve of her shoulder to mask his own shout. Pride soared through her as he hummed against her skin from his own powerful release.

He breathed hard against her and finally eased his grip, rolling to his side and wrapping his arms around her.

"Chloe, you tempt me like no other."

"Just a friendly welcome back," she said, out of breath as he eased his hand away.

He chuckled low in her ear. "And what a welcome it is."

She only had a few hours of Gage time over the weekend, and she'd already spent the first hour doing what they did best. Between both of their jobs, these stolen hours were all they had—which was good—but she took advantage while she could. The heat of his body would keep her satisfied for the dry spell to follow.

"I want more," she said. The chance to see his amazing naked body. To kiss and feel him more. All of it. She only had the weekend, and she had a big checklist to get through that involved his body and all the ways she wanted to be wrapped around it.

"Me too." He nipped her earlobe. "Especially since we have a few weeks to see where this goes."

Her eyes snapped open. "What?"

He leaned back, eyebrows raised—her reaction evidently not what he'd expected. But she couldn't help it. She rose to her feet and adjusted her clothes. Gage stood as well and buckled his belt.

"Did you say a few weeks? You're staying for that long?"

He frowned. "Yeah. I was thinking I could take you out for once and—"

"Take me out?" His words were like a bucket of ice water to the face. "Like on a date?"

He stepped so close she couldn't mistake the heat between them and tucked a lock of hair behind her ear. "I want to be with you, Chloe. Now I have time to get to know you more than one weekend at a time."

Oh God…

Her body hummed with so much need and confusion she thought she'd topple over. But she had to be honest. "Gage, I want you. You know I want you…"

He smiled and pressed against her further.

"But I don't want to date you," she finished.

When he stepped back, the look on his face made her chest tighten and her heart race.

The strong search and rescue badass of a man did not look happy.

Chapter Two

"I'm not dating him." Chloe tied a short apron around her waist and walked around the bar to get ready for the lunch rush. Living upstairs was a big plus for Chloe's nonexistent commute to work. She ran the restaurant and bar, trying to keep her mother's life's work a lucrative success. Her best friend, Natalie, had a small room for her cupcake shop off to the left-hand side of the house.

"You guys have sex every time he comes into town?" Natalie slowly applied frosting to one of her locally famous cupcakes. There was flour dusted on her apron and sweater set. She shoved her thick glasses up her nose, spreading buttercream on her face, then went back to her task.

"Well, yeah."

"Call it what you want." Natalie licked a dab of frosting off one of her fingers. "Whatever it is, it sounds like the perfect arrangement to me."

Chloe glanced at the balcony above where she'd been with Gage the night before. A tremble from the memory crept up her back. She shook it off. The upstairs was being remodeled in time for the twentieth anniversary of the restaurant, an event Chloe hoped would kick-start a busier year.

She should be focused on the remodel and anniversary. Instead, she'd spent all night wrapped in thoughts about Gage and what he wanted from her.

Natalie eyed her. "I hear he's sticking around for a while this time."

Chloe groaned—how was she going to last with him staying in town for longer than a weekend? "Depends on how unlucky I am."

Natalie shook her head. "Why do you look like that's bad news?" She placed a few chocolate shavings on the cupcake. "I can think of worse things than having him hang around."

"I can't be with him more than a night or two," Chloe mumbled. "I like our arrangement. But he wants to…take me out. You know." She glanced around, like she was worried someone would overhear them. "On a *date*."

Natalie slapped the piping bag down on the counter. "That dick! What man would have the nerve to ask a beautiful woman out on a date?"

Chloe sighed. Okay, so Natalie was giving her shit, and yeah, Chloe probably sounded crazy. But this was bad. "You know I don't do commitment, Nat."

She raised a brow. "You're committed to this place. Committed to the town and your mama's memory. I'd say you do it fine."

"I mean commitment with a man. I just…don't." The thought alone gave her hives, and even though Gage was banging in the sack—literally—three weeks was treading into dangerous waters. Because she didn't need to like him beyond their arrangement. Didn't need him, period.

At least, she didn't want to need him. She was already sold on his brand of passion. No reason to complicate things more with feelings, long term, or dating.

"Besides, you said it, I'm committed to Beaufort. Gage comes and goes. Even if I wanted more, which I don't"—unless it involved him naked—"he's not the guy."

In fact, he was the exact wrong guy. She'd seen what getting hung up waiting for her dad had done to her mother.

Working at the restaurant, honoring her mother's business and dream, those were what she took seriously. The restaurant was her home. Her career. Her life. But it had taken a dip a few years ago when her mother had gotten cancer. The famous menu she'd handcrafted had been condensed to the things Chloe knew she could provide at the same high quality, but it wasn't enough. Without her mother's passion and charm, business was slipping.

Chloe's mission was to turn Honey's around and bring back the staple foods her mother had been famous for. She wasn't going anywhere, and she also wasn't signing up for three weeks of blurred lines with Gage. She wouldn't run the risk of developing expectations when attraction was more than enough with him.

Natalie put a flour-caked hand on Chloe's shoulder. "I feel for you. And I understand. Doesn't mean I agree with your decision to stay away from the hottie. Did you see his butt?"

Chloe laughed. Yeah, she'd seen it. Gage McGraw was as fine and strong as they came.

"There's too much going on to even think about more than sex."

Natalie raised an eyebrow. "Too much going on?"

Chloe nodded. "The twentieth anniversary for the restaurant is in a couple of weeks, and I'm still adjusting to running this place."

Even though her mother had passed two years ago, Chloe still struggled to take over everything left to her. Her life was full and busy—and she was failing. She'd never be Mary

"Honey" Franklin. Her mother had been strong, kind and good at everything she tried. So sweet that everyone called her "Honey." Which was how the restaurant got its name.

Natalie leaned in. "If you know what you want, and you're set, then stick with it. Sometimes you have to cheat at his rules or play by your own."

That got Chloe's attention real quick. It made sense. She wanted Gage; Gage wanted her. Should be simple. But he was throwing this "get to know you" bit into the mix. If she wanted him, she'd have to play dirty and be prepared to run after him before he caught her and tied her to a table for dinner talk.

"I don't want to stay away from him, I just don't want to hang out with him," Chloe said.

"Well don't hold back, sweetheart," a gruff voice said behind her. Chloe turned and found Gage standing at the end of the bar. His dark eyes stared holes right through her, and she fought the urge to blush.

He was the only man who ever made her come close to feeling giddy. He had a pull on her emotions, and she needed to get them under control real quick. Because she *did* want him—as long as it was on her terms. Question was: how would she get it?

Normally she might have grabbed him and shown him how she really felt, but Easton Ambrose, the resident search and rescue EMT, had come with him. East was built like Gage, tall, strong, and good-looking. But East was the local town charmer with a playboy reputation.

Chloe knew a wingman when she saw one. Gage had come here to seduce her into romance. Well, fair was fair. If he wanted to play, she'd beat him at his own game.

"You should know by now I'm not shy about much." Chloe handed menus to both men. "Hungry?"

"Yes," Gage replied quickly. There was so much emotion in his voice. His words felt like his tongue against her skin.

"I'm starving."

"Uh…me too…but I'm going to go with a burger." East leaned back in his seat like he was waiting to see the show. "And I'll also take a cupcake," he said to Natalie. When he reached for it, Natalie slapped his hand.

"Back off, Easton, this is a work of art. Not to be pawed on."

He rolled his eyes. "Seriously, Nat?"

She looked over her cupcake, smiling and turning it to admire its perfection. "Yep."

It was no secret Natalie and Easton kind of irritated each other. Had since they were all young.

East groaned. "Why the hell do you frost them out here then if they're not for eating?"

"To drive you nuts." She smiled.

"Tempting a man with something he wants but can't have isn't very nice, you know?"

Though East might be talking about a cupcake, Chloe knew the feeling. She glanced at Gage in all his super hotness and wanted to strangle him for sitting in front of her. With all this talk about cupcakes, she wanted to steal Natalie's frosting bag and decorate her favorite dessert. Then she'd lick it off and—

She huffed out a breath and glared at the opposite wall. No point in fantasizing about what she couldn't have.

"Well, I'm off to get this in the case with the rest of them," Natalie said. "You want a cupcake, Easton? You'll have to come to my shop and buy one like everyone else." Then she pranced off with her miniature edible artwork.

"That woman needs to lighten up," East grumbled.

Now it was Chloe's turn to roll her eyes. Even though they went way back, there was no way her sweet but strictly organized rule-following BFF would lighten up anytime soon.

"Well, if you're done whining…" Chloe glanced at Gage.

"You going to order something?"

"I'd like to order you to go to dinner with me," Gage said.

She straightened her shoulders and placed her hands on her hips. Former sergeant Gage McGraw issuing an order kicked her pulse up a notch. His dominance made her want to salute and say, "Yes sir."

No! She needed to stay strong until she got what she wanted—Gage without the commitment.

"No dinner. But how about a nightcap?" she countered.

"I'm going to go put different music on the jukebox," East said. "Purely to get away from this conversation." He got up and walked across the bar to the machine.

Which gave Chloe and Gage a moment alone, and the stare down was on. Not that she cared if East heard. She wasn't ashamed of what she wanted with Gage.

Gage leaned in and put his arms on the counter. "I want a date, Chloe. Romance. And you're going to give it to me."

"Romance?" She almost dry heaved around the word. "Why is this so important to you?"

He stilled for a moment. "Because I want your time. And I'm a romantic guy."

She looked over him. He was a lot of things, mostly hard muscle and sex on a stick. But romantic? If he was serious, she was in trouble, because there wasn't a romantic bone in her body.

"Why are you fighting this?" he asked.

"Because I want your body." It was the first honest thing she could blurt out.

He raised a brow and sat back with a hint of a smile. "So you're using me for all this?" He gestured over his impressive chest encased in a black T-shirt and…oh God…camo pants. She had a thing for his tactile gear. Just the sight of him donning his big boots, butch watch, and macho swagger was enough to make her wet.

"Don't think too long, sweetheart. Would hate for the drool on the side of your mouth to get any worse."

Her face flushed. "Shut up."

"Now, I'm going to try to not take too much offence about your unwillingness to go out with me. I'll chalk it up to you being difficult."

"Well aren't you sweet," she said sarcastically.

"But I'm not about to let this slip. Because I think you kind of like me." He tossed her a wink, and damn him, she *did* kind of like him. That wasn't a secret—between the hours of sex in the past, they'd lain in bed and talked and laughed. But those were brief moments in the bedroom, and they only lasted a weekend. She could play it cool for a few hours, but a few weeks was different. All the baggage, emotions, and stuff she didn't like to think about had more time to fester and come out.

Deep down, she knew what she was capable of. She could get sucked in to all this…intimacy crap. And she didn't want to even toe the line with a guy like Gage. She'd get caught up in his smile, his body, and she'd end up wanting him in a way she couldn't. A way she *shouldn't*.

Nope. No way she'd ever show that side of herself to anyone. The only time she gave up her prized indifference was when Gage took it in the bedroom, because he knew exactly what she needed. He tapped into every desire and fantasy she had. She could be bound, at his mercy, completely taken over and totally powerful all at the same time.

She wanted—no—*needed* him to take over her body. Except he was holding his seduction hostage.

"I'm free tonight," she said. "My place. Eleven?"

He raised a brow. "Why Chloe, are you asking me over for a booty call?"

"Yes, sir, I am."

"Romantic dinner first. Seven o' clock."

She inhaled deeply. This was going to be more difficult than she thought. "Sorry, no dating. And definitely no romance."

He shrugged. "Then no sex."

"What?" she snapped, louder than she meant. Chloe cringed as people glanced in their direction. She leaned forward, lowering her voice. "You can't be serious."

"I'm completely serious, sweetheart. You give me what I want, and I'll give you what you want."

She gritted her teeth. "That's blackmail."

"It's only blackmail if you really need something and I'm withholding it for my own gain… So yeah, I guess you're right." He smiled. "It *is* blackmail."

He was being cute now because he knew how badly she needed his body. It'd been four months, and last night's *welcome back* had only awakened her need. And now he was right in front of her—her own personal gourmet cupcake— teasing her with terms she wouldn't fulfill.

Cheat at his rules or make your own…

She eyed him and raised her chin. "You wanna play, city boy? Looks like we'll see who will outlast whom." She ran her eyes over his impressive body—he was looking her up and down right back. "Seems I'm not the only one with a drooling problem."

His eyes darted to hers. Finally, she had some kind of upper hand. Yes, he wanted romance, but he also wanted her. And she knew enough of his ticks to tempt the roughened man into seeing things her way.

She leaned over the bar, her cleavage all but spilling out over the top of her tank—Gage's gaze dropped right where she wanted it—and she grinned.

"Like it or not, we both know last night wasn't enough," she said. "You want more, like I do. You want to blackmail me? Fine. But don't think I won't retaliate."

He leaned in until his mouth was hovering over hers. "I expect nothing less."

That stubborn, sexy woman was driving him insane. It was only his third day back in town, and he was already busting at the seams of both his patience and his damn pants.

"Here is an example of stomped-on underbrush," Gage said to the team of search and rescue volunteers. East—his closest friend, besides Chloe—was at his side, helping him educate the new volunteers for basic training. The fun stuff would come later in the week, when they'd take the main team to the next level of Sartec training. He had to get his shit together quick or he wouldn't be able to do his job.

Yesterday at the bar, Chloe had made it clear she was going to fight him on this romance idea. She knew what she was doing to him, and part of him liked the challenge. He wanted to know her more, and not just because she was different, sassy, and equipped with enough attitude to whip him so hard he could taste it. But when the rope had loosened and his grip had slipped—when he'd started falling—he'd thought of her.

Her eyes. Her face. How she looked so damn beautiful in the early morning light before sunrise. He'd spent hours watching shadows play over her face as she slept, and he always hated watching the clock count down to the end of their amazing weekends.

Did she miss him? Were the few details they knew about each other enough for her? It wasn't enough for him—not even close. He wanted more of her, in every way—and he wanted her to know him back. Because she was the closest thing to an honest-to-God connection he had.

He needed to know if a relationship was even possible.

Sure, it'd be long distance, but he'd come back here whenever he could if he had Chloe to come home to.

He didn't want to think about what he'd do if this gambit failed. When it came to an S&R, he was prepared for the worst. When it came to being rejected by the one woman he'd ever wanted? He didn't know what he'd do. Fortunately, he had a group of trainees to take his mind off Chloe.

He pointed to the shrubs and the ground. "The prints and the broken bushes show someone came through here."

The volunteers nodded, and East looked them over while Gage gave his lecture. The local team was a damn fine one, but with the new recruits coming in, they needed to get up to speed quickly. There were a lot of acres in the area to cover, and Beaufort's S&R team handled the greater Carolina area. As soon as an S&R call came in, he'd be out there saving people, but in the meantime, he'd be damned if he didn't make sure these new recruits were beyond ready for duty.

"Let's call it a day," East said.

Gage didn't argue. It was broaching sundown, and he was ready for dinner…which he'd be having alone, apparently. He hadn't stopped thinking of Chloe for a damn second. She was right, he wanted her. Bad.

"You all right?" East asked. "You look like someone pissed in your Wheaties."

Gage scoffed. "Nope, just a certain woman pissing me off is all."

East nodded.

"Yeah, I've known Chloe for a long time," East said. "You sure you know what you're doing? She can be vicious when she wants something."

Chloe, East, and Natalie had been childhood friends forever. Nothing romantic, but East probably knew Chloe better than he did. Something Gage was a bit jealous of.

"I'm aware of how vicious she can be. But she's fighting

mostly to irritate me."

"Or she really doesn't want to date you."

Gage nailed him with a glare. "Bullshit."

"All I'm saying, man, is you really want her for more than your arrangement, it's going to be tough. You two have been doing this for what? A year?"

"Two," Gage said. Which was why he believed they were capable of more. Who stayed fuck buddies for two years? Most moved on to the next person so they could keep it casual. "Christ, all I'm asking for is a meal and conversation before we take our clothes off, but she's acting like I'm proposing marriage."

"Aw, cute. You want to cuddle and talk about your feelings and she only wants to fuck. Must be rough being you."

"Shut up," Gage said. He was aware of how this looked, and frankly he didn't give a damn. Yes, he wanted Chloe so fucking much he could taste it. But he also wanted to hear her laugh like she had the last time they'd stayed up all night, getting lost in each other's body, then talking, then doing it all over again.

But he was too far in now. He had to stick to his guns. No matter how hard—literally—it was.

He pulled out his phone and shot her a quick text.

Dinnertime is coming up…have you seen reason yet? I'm hungry, sweetheart, and we both know you are, too.

In a few seconds, his phone pinged back with a text from Chloe.

I'll see your dinner and offer up "a quick meal" instead.

He grinned. She was already caving. But he'd hold strong. Romance for sex. But a quick meal for some messing around could take the edge off…

Deal.

His phone pinged again.

Great. Why don't you come get me in an hour?

His fingers worked fast to reply: *I'll be there.*

With that, his evening was looking up and a sexy woman was in his future.

Chapter Three

Chloe tried not to cackle with pride as she went about setting up her "quick meal" to share with Gage. But she really wanted to pat herself on the back for being so clever. She never said anything about leaving her house to get their dinner.

The restaurant was in full swing downstairs, and her crew of wonderful employees was overseeing it while she attended to very important business. Her living space was on the third floor and had a private entrance around back, which Gage had used several times.

She glanced at the clock. He would be there soon, and the process for this meal was a carefully structured one. Hopefully when Gage walked in and saw what she'd prepared, he'd forget the silly date idea and give her what she wanted.

She carefully placed some well-crafted finger foods down and smiled.

Yeah…this was going to be good.

G age climbed the private stairwell up to Chloe's apartment above the large Victorian house. The closer he got, the more he could smell the familiar scent of her home. Warm apples mixed with fresh ocean air and a subtle spring flower that was all her. He didn't know exactly what home smelled like, but he was pretty sure that was it.

He knocked on her door. He'd showered and shaved, and if he were honest, he was excited she had finally accepted his offer. Good thing, too. As it was, he was already hurting for a sample of her. Every muscle in his body begged to be unleashed. He needed to wrap her up. Pin her down. Make her beg.

He knocked again.

"It's unlocked!" Chloe's muffled yell came from inside.

Gage opened the door. He walked in, shut the door behind him, and locked it. He'd need to have a talk with her about safety. A single woman leaving her door unlocked at night wasn't wise.

"Chloe?" he called out. The living room was dark, but around the corner came a soft glowing light from the dining room.

"In here," she called. Gage hadn't been in her home in four months, but everything looked the same. Clean, colorful, and well lived in. He made his way to the dining room—

And froze. Every damn cell in his body shot to high alert at the sight of what lay before him.

"Ready for your quick meal, city boy?" she asked.

Jee-sus Christ.

He blew out a breath and looked her over. She was completely naked, lying on her long dining room table, with perfectly placed bits of fruit and pastries covering her most delicious parts.

He stared. This was fucking incredible, and his cock agreed. He didn't want a quick meal. He wanted to devour her.

Gage stepped toward her, zeroing in on the sweets and strawberries covering her nipples. He'd never wanted to lick anything as bad as he did right then. She'd even somehow dipped the tips of her perfect breasts in sugar.

"Hope you're still hungry," she purred.

Oh hell yeah he was hungry. She was perfect. Alabaster skin with the soft light making her glow like fresh cream. Her green eyes were fixed on him, and her breaths increased with every step he took toward her.

Wait. This… This was what she wanted. This was *exactly* what she wanted.

"Well played, sweetheart," he growled. She'd lured him in and played him. To her credit, it was fucking brilliant—she was taking Candy Land to the next level. But still. A game was a game, and she had messed with the rules.

"Whatever do you mean?" she asked innocently. "It's a quick meal. Technically, this counts."

He shook his head. Fine. If this was her hand, he'd throw down his cards and play, too.

"Sorry, sugar tits." He leaned over and snagged one slice of strawberry from her breast with his teeth, purposefully biting her nipple a little in the process. She gasped, and he ran his fingers down her stomach to the peach slices covering her mound. "I wanted a dinner date for sex. This is—"

"Technically a dinner date," she growled.

"No." He bent over again to snag a peach slice. He sucked it into his mouth and lingered between her folds to get the hint of her taste. Damn, he missed this. Missed her. "This is a quick meal. You said so yourself."

He grabbed another slice of peach and circled it around her clit, then dipped it between her folds like an apple into caramel. She moaned and arched her back slightly.

"I really do love finger foods." He popped the slice into

his mouth—her sweetness on the fruit was his new favorite dessert.

"I'm glad," she whispered. "Have as much as you want."

Oh, he would. He'd just have to find a way to refrain from taking every last inch of her to the brink and back.

"Appetizers aren't a full meal though." He slid his finger inside her to hammer home his point. "Our deal was sex for a romantic dinner date." He slowly withdrew. "So this would be finger foods for…" He thrust back inside, and she moaned.

With two slices of peach gone and her pretty core exposed for him, he wanted to lean in and taste her again, but this was an even exchange. Finger foods for finger play. So he withdrew, then pumped back inside her again. He hooked his fingers, hitting the spot inside that drove her wild, and her back arched farther.

"Since it's a quick meal, you should meet me halfway," she pleaded.

He raised a brow. "You think so?"

She nodded spastically. Poor woman was trembling. And he was fighting the need to give her exactly what she wanted. Maybe he could compromise.

He dipped his head again, snagged another peach, then chewed it until juice ran along his mouth. He spread her legs even wider and sucked hard on her clit—her sweetness, mixed with the bite of fruit, brought a whole new meaning to peaches and cream.

She grabbed the edges of the table. "Oh yes!"

Fuck! He forced himself to back away. Fingers only.

"What are you doing?" she asked.

"Playing fair." He slowly worked his fingers in and out. "You're the one who started this with *finger* foods."

He thrust deep again, and she groaned. He might not be able to take her with his cock, or his mouth, but he'd take her with his hand.

She arched, and some strawberries fell away from her breasts, leaving sugar-coated ruby tipped nipples straining for the ceiling. She was his personal dessert, and he wanted to eat every inch. But he couldn't. Not without breaking his own rules.

"Please take me, Gage," she pleaded softly.

Truth was, he had a hard time denying her—he wanted nothing more than to give her exactly what she wanted. But he had to keep his focus. He was playing the long game.

"I'll give you what you need." He pressed his thumb against her sensitive bundle of nerves. "If you give me what I want."

Her head lolled back and forth on the table. She was either shaking her head or delirious with pleasure. He hoped the latter.

"Come on, sweetheart. We both know you want to…" He plucked another peach slice with his mouth, careful not to lick her this time. The effort damn near killed him.

"Mouth," she begged.

He rubbed his thumb against her sweet spot faster. "Can't," he rasped. "The exchange is fingers for fingers, not oral for oral."

"Okay!" she moaned. "Deal. Oral for oral."

He slowed his pace enough to keep her on the brink of coming while he negotiated his terms.

"Oral romance for oral sex? Tell me how you plan to accomplish that, sweetheart."

"I can say sweet things to you if you stop talking and use your mouth to do dirty things to me."

He chuckled. She was fiery and begging and damn it, he wanted to agree. It'd stay within the rules…

"I'm waiting for my romance then. I'm ready to hear you whisper sweet nothings to me." He surged two fingers in deep, and she gasped. "And you better mean them."

"Oh yes, please Gage."

"Mmm, I love it when you see it my way." He pulled up a chair and sat at the end of the table. He tugged her toward him until her ass hung off the edge, tossed her legs over his shoulders, brought her as close as possible, and blew against her hotness. She moaned, and her thighs tensed by his ears.

"Comp-compromise," she stuttered out. "I'll give you your sweet nothings, but I have one demand."

He laughed and blew again against her heated flesh. "Of course you do. Especially since you're the one at my mercy. By all means, make your demands."

She lifted herself up on her hands, and the bits of fruit left on her slid down her sides and slapped against the table. "I want to make you come. It's been so long. Please."

That was the nail in his coffin. This sexy mastermind of a woman wanted to make him come? That was her demand? He'd be lying if he wasn't hell of fucking interested.

"Quickie for a quickie?" he asked.

She grinned and nodded. "Doesn't break either of our standpoints, and we both get a little something to tide us over. What do you say, city boy?"

He was ready to say fuck it, climb up on the table, and remind her who worked her body to the point of sweaty bliss. Instead, he'd stick to his rules and the one card he had to play: her body. He still had sex in his arsenal, and he wouldn't trade it until all his demands were met.

"Let me think for a second." He bit the inside of her thigh. "I'm still waiting for my sweet nothings."

"You bastard." She groaned.

"Hmmm…" He ran his nose up her thigh. "I think you're confused on what sweet words entail."

She blew out a breath. "Roses are red, violets are blue—"

He nipped her mound and she yipped.

"I told you to mean it," he said.

"I was going to say you're super hot and I want your cock, too. But you ruined my poetry."

"Try again." He hovered over her pulsing clit, hoping he could outlast her. As it was, he was ready to dive in and drink her down until he couldn't see straight.

"I like the way you look at me," she whispered.

He glanced up her body and met her eyes, silently coaxing her to continue.

"I like the feel of your arms against my skin when you hug me. When you wrap them around me. I feel…small."

He kept his gaze on hers and slowly trailed his tongue along her clit. She smiled and arched into him.

"You're the only man I've gone back to more than once," she admitted around a breathless moan of bliss.

Her words were more addicting than the sugar on her skin. He wanted to tell her how amazing she was, but that's not what she wanted. So he delved his tongue deep and gave her what she did want.

She moaned and her arms shook.

He smiled and pulled back. "Lie down, sweetheart. I've got you. I'll even make it quick."

She lowered herself flat against the table. The sound of her skin sticking to the surface as her back met the wood flared a dose of need in him, hot and quick. Every breath, gasp, and move she made was like a siren calling. Those same damn breaths would linger in his ears long after she was gone and echo in his dreams.

"You drive me crazy," she said. "I've never known another man like you."

He licked faster, flicking wildly until her back was arching.

"Oh God…" she moaned. "Never known another man who can make me feel the way you do."

He was deep in paradise, surrounded by her smooth skin and silky core, and he didn't want to be anywhere else. Her heels dug into his back, and she worked her hips up and down, fucking his tongue every time he thrust it deep.

She was so close. So responsive. His to maneuver how he wanted. She challenged his strength, but bringing her to heel was hot, and he was a bastard for loving it the way he did. And her words—he wanted to beg her to repeat them. Because his hope of convincing her to try a long-distance relationship lay in those words. Maybe his exchange of romance for sex could pay off in the end and he'd get what he wanted.

Her.

For now, he'd stick to the rules. Play the game. An even exchange.

He ate her like he'd never get the chance again. She was drenching his tongue. Raining down on him. Her sheath tensed and the table creaked as she squirmed against his mouth. She was there.

"Ready to come for me?"

"Yes!" She threw her hips out, and he knew what she wanted. She wanted to be filled. She liked it hard and rough and deep. He ran his hand down his jeans where his cock was straining against the fabric—God, it'd feel incredible to have it buried deep in her…

But all he could do was yank her closer and drive his tongue deep once, twice, three times. And then, when she was panting, he pulled back and surged a finger inside.

Her ass came off the table, but his mouth was right there to catch her clit, lock down, and suck the little bundle while thrusting a finger in and out.

She wiggled and trembled. Her hands slapped on the table, and she threw her hips up to rub even harder against his lips. And right then, Gage was teetering on the brink of losing himself.

Fire.
        Chloe was certain Gage had replaced her blood with fire.

Every stroke of his tongue and pump of his hand had her burning up from the inside out. She was so close, yet so far. She was getting what she wanted…sort of. She loved sex. Loved feeling him inside her, and he knew it. He could make her come so easily, and he would. But she always wanted the extra feeling of his naked body against hers, inside hers. Loved feeling his skin, his cock, his muscles.

What was that called? Connection?

No, no, surely not. And even if it was, she wouldn't admit it.

This was an even exchange, pure and simple. She had to say things to get what she wanted. Sure, everything she'd told him was true, but that didn't mean she wanted to embrace anything beyond a few sweet words. Certainly not "the romance" he kept demanding.

A burst of pleasure jolted through her body when he sucked harder and buried another finger deep, curving it to rub continuously over the sensitive spot inside her.

Those flames erupted and roared, flooding her body like a tidal wave that grew and swelled until finally—

Raw pleasure surged and slammed into her like pulsing water crashing into the shore. "Yes!" she screamed.

He drank her down, working his tongue a bit slower, as if savoring her release on his fingers and lips. Her whole body shook, and the table against her back squeaked as she convulsed.

More. She needed more. The bad thing about Gage was every time she was with him, she never felt sated, only more crazed. As if the first orgasm had only awakened a deeper need only he could satisfy.

Chloe got up, slid off the table, and straddled his lap. She wrapped her arms around his neck and kissed him hard. She needed to feel him. Experience him. She'd waited so damn long, and now she had him right where she wanted him. She reached between them and fumbled with his belt. Unzipped his pants. In one quick move, she'd have his cock free and inside her—

"Easy there," he growled. He pulled on her hair until it stung, thrusting her chin in the air before he claimed her mouth with his.

She grabbed his hair, too, pulling him into a deeper kiss, and went for the glory. She pushed her hands into his underwear—

He pulled her hand back out and meshed her fingers with his.

"Ah, ah. This was a fair exchange. No full sex until I get full romance. My demands stand. You ready for our dinner date?"

She growled and glared at him. He was right there, so hard he was pulsing.

Gage tugged her hair a little more, and she gasped. "Don't go being a poor sport because you didn't get your way." He nipped her chin.

"I still want to make you come." She looked at him while his grip held firm in her hair. She was at his mercy. They both knew it. She might not be able to get into his pants the way she wanted, but maybe she could work around them.

She slowly sank her hand into his open fly and gripped his rock-hard shaft through his boxers. His jaw clenched.

"Looks like the vote is two"—she squeezed his cock—"to one. Me and this big guy here are all for some fun. You're the only one playing coy."

He breathed deep, as if trying to gain composure, but she had him. With his fingers still in her hair and her hand on his cock, she maneuvered her way off his lap and hit her knees between his spread legs. Halfway down, his grip on her hair tightened. Tough guy wanted to come as badly as she wanted him to.

And God did she want to make him come. The sooner she felt him surge from her touch, the sooner she could slake this aching need.

One thing she liked about Gage was how he made her feel different. She could be honest. Give in to her fantasies and let passion rule. There was no overthinking, because the time they shared never lasted long enough to really overthink.

Until this recent stunt of his with the whole three week sticking around thing. Too much time led to too much thinking and too many opportunities for the fantasy to dwindle. She wanted to stay in suspended bliss with him. Was that so much to ask?

Truth was, she'd rather be a momentary fantasy than a heartbroken reality.

A spike of anger hit her at his insistence on breaking through the boundaries that kept her safe and satisfied enough to keep moving forward.

She pulled his pants low on his hips and tugged his cock out. Finally, she had all the access she needed. He was driving her crazy by denying her what she wanted, but maybe it was time to turn the tables.

Sex for romance? Nope.

But oral for oral? He had no idea what he was getting himself into.

"So now that you've gotten your sweet nothings, time for the dirty talk," she said. "And since you're in the spirit of an even exchange, you're going to sit there and take it. Because I have you at my mercy now."

"Chloe…"

"You asked me the other night what I thought of?" she purred in her best seductress voice while keeping a tight grip on the base of his cock. "I've thought of this…" She ran her tongue along the crown, and he hissed. "I thought of how good you taste. How good you feel." She closed her mouth over the head and sucked hard, then delivered a little kiss to ease the sting. "I'd make myself come just picturing sucking you. I'd think of every detail I could remember, every ridge and inch of you."

She licked down the entire shaft, then up the other side. His hips subtly flexed, coaxing her for more.

"So good…" he murmured.

"And you want to hear a secret?" She hovered her mouth over where he wanted it most. "I'd suck my own fingers, imagining it was you, while sinking the others inside of me." She put her free hand between her legs. "Like this." She took his entire length into her throat while matching the action with her own finger disappearing inside of her.

"Jesus, Chloe." He moved his hips with her, matching her intake with a thrust upward.

She stole glances at his expression. His head fell back, but his gaze never strayed from her for long. Holding her face, he ran his thumbs along her cheekbones and over her hollowing cheeks as she worked him up and down with her mouth.

"I've thought of this so many damn times," he said. "But my imagination is never as good as the real thing."

That made her want to preen. The sexy, sinister man could easily break her, consume her, and he was clutching her like he needed a place to fall. She loved this power she had over him, but she wanted more. Always more. It was a need she wasn't sure would ever pass, so she'd take what she could. It was the basis of what made their casual relationship work.

Just taking what I can, while I can…

She'd repeat it over and over if she had to. There was a time cap, because she couldn't do weeks of dating and romance with him. But this? She sucked him deeper, pumped the base of his cock. *This* she could do. Feeling him tense and hum beneath her mouth was what she wanted. To make him feel pleasure like no one else could, and for him to do the same to her.

But still, getting in too deep with him was dangerous, which was why brief interactions were best.

She pumped faster. Sucked hard at the tip, then drew his entire cock into her mouth, in and out, in and out, again and again. A low groan escaped his chest as she licked the big vein that climbed up his shaft.

Her only complaint was his clothes. They were still on.

It was a crime for anything to cover his impressive muscles. All she could see was the hint of his powerful thighs showing. His naked body put Adonis to shame, and she couldn't even get more than a glimpse. That needed to change.

She removed her hand from between her legs and went to lift his shirt. But he caught her wrist and brought that finger to his mouth and sucked it.

"Mmm, fuck, I could eat you forever." He licked her finger clean and delivered a little bite. She grazed her teeth along his flesh as his balls drew up. "I'm there, I'm going to come."

She bore down, sucking faster and faster. With a tight grip on her wrist, he bit down on the fleshy part of her thumb as his release hit the back of her throat.

She swallowed him down and continued sucking until he shuddered and collapsed backward, saved only by her grabbing his shirt and holding him in place. When she let him go, he slowly sat up and planted kisses along her knuckles and fingertips.

"You can't make this easy, can you?" He tucked a lock of hair behind her ear.

She clung to his open pants resting low on his hips, and she looked up into those intense eyes. "I want you to stay.

I want to feel you inside me. Want you to take me hard and slow, then rough and fast. Stay tonight and I promise I'll be extremely easy."

He kissed her lips lightly and whispered, "Have dinner with me. One date. And I'll be easy right back."

She looked up into those eyes and her knees swayed. But she had to stay strong. Gage was dangerous for her heart—she'd known that from day one. Time wasn't on her side—the more she fell, the more it would hurt. And she knew better than to expect too much. They had a powerful, explosive sexual relationship. Pretending they had anything more was a disaster waiting to happen.

He knew that. She knew that. It was only a question of how long he could resist her. But sooner or later, he'd give up this crazy scheme of his. She just had to be hot, tempting… and patient.

She gave a small tug on his pants and fastened them.

He glanced down and nodded. Her answer was clear.

"This isn't over." He kissed her hard and quick. "Not by a long shot."

He turned and stomped out and her body broke out into goose bumps. She knew very well she was poking a bear, and yes…this wasn't over by a long shot.

Chapter Four

"God, this sucks so bad." Chloe tossed her spatula on the counter. She'd woken up early to try to make her mom's famous crab cakes and test them out as a specialty appetizer for next week's twentieth anniversary of the restaurant.

"It's not *so* bad…" Natalie looked over her shoulder in the big back kitchen of the restaurant. Chloe didn't have to turn around to feel her frowning. "Are they supposed to be black?"

Chloe shook her head. "No."

What would her mom think if she could see the restaurant now? They were making do, sure, but they were nowhere near the level of perfection her mother had achieved. She could imagine her restaurant ending up on a show like *Kitchen Nightmares*. Once great, now in steady decline, soon to vanish from the face of the earth.

No, she'd die before she let that happen. This wasn't just a great restaurant—it was all she had left of her mother. People came and went, but this? Just this once, Chloe would get it right.

Which was why she'd hired a chef. It was also why this twentieth anniversary event needed to have her mother's old recipes reinstated—and furthermore, why *she* had to be the one to bring them back.

The other foods set to go on the menu were close to perfect—thanks to said amazing chef—but Chloe wanted to make this one dish herself. Crab cakes had been her favorite thing to eat growing up, comfort food when her dad had left, a bittersweet solace when her mom had gotten sick.

Her mom had insisted on making them for her even when her health had declined and she should have been resting in bed. Chloe had never been able to recreate their uniquely delicious flavors, but she was determined to try. It was the one thing she wanted to make and present. Anything to feel closer to her mother and prove that to herself she was a part of her goodness.

"The anniversary party is next week." Chloe scraped the pan, and it spit oil at her. "And these aren't going on the menu until they're right."

Natalie gently patted Chloe's shoulder. "Keep trying."

Chloe spun to face her. "You're a chef. Can't you help me? Teach me something? Anything."

"Whoa, I *bake*. Big difference." Natalie shoved her glasses up her nose, then peered back at the pan. "Besides, don't think I forgot you telling me to leave you alone and let you do it yourself."

Oh, right, that. Last week she might have snipped at her best friend. She'd never meant to, but frustration was running high, and if there was one thing Chloe hated, it was being so close to something and not finishing.

Her mind briefly turned to Gage.

Talk about frustrating.

But this dish had to be right, and she had to do it. No

failing. No "coming close." Nope, this had to be perfect. Her mother was dead, and honestly, Chloe had watched her die in more ways than one over the years. First, she'd watched her soul slowly wither after her father left them. Then she watched cancer slowly take her body. The two things in her life she'd never been able to control…death and being left.

On a deep breath and rapid batting of her lashes to keep the sting away, she looked at her friend.

"I'm not saying make the crab cakes for me. I'm saying maybe give me a hint or two."

Natalie raised an eyebrow. "Snap my fingers and turn you into Gordon Ramsay for a day?" She chuckled. "I don't think it works that way." She hugged Chloe, then stepped back and held her shoulders. "You have to believe you're capable of something more. Trust yourself. The anniversary will be great and the restaurant will be packed."

Yeah, it would be. And she hoped her mother would be proud. It'd only been two years since she'd passed away and it still hurt. She'd been the kindest woman in the world, and her spirit had never broken—except when it came to Chloe's father. He'd crushed Mary Franklin in a way no one and nothing else could. She'd waited for him to return until her dying breath.

Chloe had met Gage right after her mother had passed, and he'd been the best distraction. But with the anniversary of the restaurant coming up and Gage in town, her mother's presence and all the sadness and joy that came with it lingered in her mind. She tried to stay positive, but lately she was sure she was failing her mother's memory. Failing her business. Failing to live up to the legacy her mother had left behind.

"Did the article come out yet?" Natalie asked.

The local newspaper had done an article featuring Honey's and a retrospective on how her mother had turned her own home into the bar and grill twenty years ago. The journalist had promised the article would run this week, but still nothing.

"No. I'm keeping an eye out for it."

Natalie nodded and hopped up on the counter, dangling her legs against the cabinets. "So...are you going to tell me about last night with hottie McSearchy?"

Chloe grabbed a potholder and hustled the sizzling pan to the sink. "It was fine."

"Uh-huh. Is that why you look equal parts mad and happy?"

She sighed. "I got *some* of what I wanted."

"Some? Tough cookie to swallow when your heart is set on the whole batch." Natalie winked. "So he didn't give up the man meat, huh?"

"Jesus," Chloe said around a smile. "Did you seriously say 'man meat'?"

"What? I'm just asking."

"We messed around," Chloe said. "But no *main course*."

"Ah, rough."

Tell me about it.

That ache to feel Gage's skin against hers—to lock her legs around him as he buried himself inside her over and over—was becoming overwhelming. She was getting cranky waiting for him to give up on the *romance* thing and give in to the lust that'd gotten them this far.

"I mean, the other stuff is good and last night was great." Her face warmed—one recollection of his tongue and feeling him deep in her throat was all it took to get her worked up. "I just want sex. Is that so wrong?"

"You're preaching to the caterer," Natalie said.

Chloe raised a brow. "Really?"

"What? It's so hard to believe I want a fun sweaty night of...of..." She frowned at the ground, searching for the word.

"Passion?" Chloe offered.

Natalie snapped her finger, her big eyes wide. "Yes! Passion."

Oh boy. Maybe Chloe should stop bitching, because the one thing she had with Gage was passion. So much it freaked her out.

"He wants romance. A date." Chloe shuddered.

"But until he gets his romance, he's not putting out?"

"Yep." Chloe sighed. After last night, it was clear Gage would only give her as much as she gave him. The longer she was hell bent against romance, the longer she'd go without sex. Unless there was a way to break him.

"Well, while you're busy not having sex, I'm going to my shop to not have sex either. Wanna do girls night later this week and we can drown our celibate sorrows in some Rocky Road while watching a Nick Sparks movie?"

"Sounds like a date," Chloe said, which was the most hypocritical thing she could have said. There she stood, not having sex with a man she wanted to have sex with while the smell of burned food and irritation crept in around her.

She was not caving. Not developing feelings. Not giving in.

Nope…she was perfectly fine.

The pan hissed at her as if sensing her mood. So she scowled back and crossed her arms.

"Perfectly fine."

Gage zipped his pack and glanced out the window of his temporary office—a rustic cabin in the forestry department. The team was waiting on him so they could continue their training. But all he could think about was the other night with Chloe.

She was going to send him to his grave with a permanent

hard-on and enough cold showers under his belt to start a drought in North Carolina. She was smart and sexy, and out of all the women he'd met, she was the only one who challenged him on a level that made him stand up and take notice.

He knew what she was doing. She was stringing him along, hoping he'd give up and give in. Little did she know that the more they played this game, the more determined he was to win.

A little distance from her, however, had given him enough space to think. After all…what in the world would he do if she ever gave him what he wanted? He wanted to try the romance thing with her for at least a night to get an idea of what it'd be like.

And if she *did* agree to something where they expected more than hot sex whenever he happened to come through town? Then he just hoped she'd agree that a long-distance relationship was best. He couldn't give up the independence that let him rescue anyone wherever duty called him. He had to be able to go wherever someone needed him.

The glimpse he'd gotten into her mind all the times he'd been here before left him wanting more. He wasn't a fan of the no-sex thing, but one meal, one date to look at her and see her in a new way wouldn't be so bad. Maybe then they'd both know if this was worth pursuing.

Yet she pushed back at every attempt he made.

She had said sweet things to him, though. Score one point for him.

The woman was irritating at worst and sexy as hell at best. And that was just scratching the surface. There was a lot more to Chloe Franklin. And that was what Gage was trying to get to.

He knew her mom had died a couple of years ago, and he knew that they'd been very close.

He replayed the first few times he'd been with Chloe.

She'd clung to him, and there'd been a sadness in her. He'd felt it in her every touch, in every plea she gave him to be touched back. He'd only found out later that her mom had died so soon before Chloe had hooked up with him, and it had been then that he realized why she'd been so hungry to lose herself in his arms. Why she'd consumed him and begged to be consumed in return.

He'd tried asking her about it the next time he came into town, but she'd shut him up with a kiss on his mouth and a hand on his cock.

So he had come up with unique ways to get her to open up without her knowing. Asking basic, simple questions that gave insight to her deeper feelings. Like how she loved chocolate but only ate it when she was stressed or sad. She'd eaten a lot of chocolate after her mother had died. But still, she'd never opened up to him about it. Or about her life.

He'd had women open up to him from day one in a ploy to pin him down, but it was the one who wouldn't let him in who'd hooked him from moment one.

And he was sure now that she liked him. And damn it, he liked her—she was perfect for him. Well. Almost. He had to break past her aversion to romance first.

But…what if he couldn't?

He shook his head. No, he still had time. He could wear her down and show her having a relationship built around more than sex wasn't so bad.

"You about ready?" East walked in, fully geared up, just like Gage was. Camo, painted face, pack strapped to his back, tools and weapons at the ready.

Enough about romance—Gage was looking forward to today. He'd rather be out in the field, but while waiting for the next mission, he'd busy himself taking a new Search & Rescue team through difficult drills. Come hell or high water, they'd be ready. And if they weren't? He'd be there with them to pick up the slack.

First order of business: take the recruits through a mock rescue. The guys would go out, follow the clues East and Gage had set up, then finally find the mock victim. Gage and East were in camo in order to stay hidden while following and watching the team's performance. The team in training was in bright orange so they'd be easy to spot while they completed the mock rescue.

"You're going to cover the first quadrant," Gage said. "I've got the second. Boys should find the checkpoint in a few hours."

Going into bear country on a ten-mile hike of unforgiving terrain was exactly what he needed. At least he hoped it'd be enough to take his mind off Chloe.

East smiled. "Still thinking about her, huh?"

Shit, was he that transparent?

"Just getting ready." He gave the zipper on his pack a final tug.

"Uh-huh. So you're still not getting any."

Technically he was getting plenty. He just wasn't getting what he wanted. Which was worse, because it left him wanting a hell of a lot more. Christ, he could still taste her. Feel her smooth skin and the hint of peaches as he ate the most perfect fruit slices he'd ever had.

"You're her friend. Why is she so damn stubborn?"

East shrugged. "She doesn't do commitment."

"I gathered," Gage grumbled. "But it's not like I'm asking for a ton of time. Just more than a weekend."

And if that worked, maybe more. But he couldn't present the idea of a long-distance relationship to Chloe when she gagged over the notion of a single date. But if she'd go on one date, they'd know how well they worked together in *and* out of the bedroom.

So fine. He'd wear her down and give her a bit of sex in

exchange for romance.

"Anything longer than a weekend could be considered a lot of time to her," East said. "Besides, what's your end game here?"

"To get to know Chloe better."

"Yeah, but you're leaving as soon as the next mission calls."

"I always leave." Gage hesitated. "But I could come back more often. Stay for a bit longer when I do. Circumstances depending."

East raised an eyebrow. "Yeah? What kind of circumstances?"

"Chloe."

"Oh, I thought you were going to say you could work here. Like maybe training full-time. We could use a head of S&R for emergency services in North Carolina. You could be stationed here in Beaufort."

Gage almost laughed. East had never been the subtle type, but he ought to know better than to try to tempt Gage with something he'd never wanted in the first place.

"No thanks." He didn't stay anywhere too long—it was in his DNA to be in the field. Physically doing something, helping. As soon as the next mission came, he'd be long gone. What kind of man would he be if he only took missions locally? What if someone needed him four states away? He'd never be able to sleep at night if someone died after he hadn't gone there himself.

"I'm here until the next mission," he said. "Don't get any ideas."

"Well then why are you trying to date Chloe if you're always going to leave?"

"People make things work. A lot of couples work around jobs that keep them busy in other states. Just think about military families when someone's deployed."

The difference was he could come back to Beaufort—and Chloe—on his down time. He'd have someone to come home to. If she'd ever go for it.

"But none of this really matters right now," Gage went on. "She can't seem to stay around me for longer than a couple of hours, so—"

"So you figured you'd use your layover to test it out," East finished. "And convince her of your grand plan while you're at it. Tactical approach."

Why was he saying that like it was a bad thing? It was smart—and yes, tactical. So what?

"Either way, more time equals more commitment," East finally said. "Staying or going, it all comes back to you asking for something neither of you ever thought was an option. Hell, something neither of you *wanted* to be an option."

Until he'd almost dropped off the side of a cliff. "People change."

"Yeah. You happen to tell her what inspired *you* to change?"

Gage crossed his arms. "She won't even go on a date with me. You want me to tell her she was my last thought when I was about to die?"

"Sincerity wouldn't be the worst idea."

Gage looked away. Maybe he'd tell her his secret one day, but now? He wasn't an idiot. He couldn't open up to her like that.

Better to focus on what they were good at and build from there. They already did the coming and going thing so well. Taking their relationship to the next level wouldn't be so bad, would it?

A date with her would be the start of something real. Because no matter how many places he'd traveled, Chloe felt the most welcoming. The warmest. The most like home.

East raised his eyebrows. "So basically, you want some

kind of commitment."

Yes! A commitment was exactly what he wanted—but Gage shrugged. "I'm open to it."

"Ah, but guess who hates commitment?" East teased.

And they were back to square one.

East's phone pinged with a text message, but he didn't answer it. Instead, his friend looked him dead in the eye. "Trying to convince a woman who hates commitment to wait around for you isn't going to go over well. But hey, I'm not a romantic like you."

Gage shook his head. His plan was solid, he just had to stick to it. Staying in one place too long made him restless. He was meant to move, to search and seek out, which was why he was so good at his job. But he wanted to come back to Chloe. That counted for something, didn't it?

"Chloe knows I move around a lot," he said. "She'll be fine if I'm upfront about what she's getting into."

"So let me get this straight." East scratched the side of his jaw. "You can commit to a woman but not a place, and she can commit to a place but not a man?"

Gage's eyes shot wide. If that wasn't the fucking shit of it. Beaufort was Chloe's hometown. The few times they'd talked in the past, she'd mentioned her mother had lived here…and died here. That one thing alone gave Chloe a connection to this place Gage had never experienced.

For this to work, he'd have to convince Chloe to give him a more committed long-distance relationship. If she was okay with him coming and going, surely, in time, he could convince her to take their relationship to the next level. Right?

Mission accepted.

"I still think this could work," Gage said, liking this renewed vigor for convincing Chloe to date him. "It's a matter of showing up and proving the benefits."

Either way, it was a win-win. No matter how he spun it,

it all boiled down to getting to know her wants and needs better. He just wanted to know when he came back from each mission, she'd be there ready to welcome him home—and not as a booty call. He wanted to be near her. Have a connection. Someone to have dinner with and wake up to every morning.

East chuckled. "The benefits to a committed-sporadic-long-distance relationship. But in the meantime, you're going to continue your recon mission on Chloe whether or not she's willing to give you a commitment." He punched Gage's arm. "Good luck."

Gage's eyes widened. Christ, when East said it like that, it sounded terrible. All he was trying to do was gather information and get the best outcome possible. "It's not like *that…*"

East adjusted his pack on his shoulder. "You know there's another way to go about this."

Gage lifted a brow in question.

"You could be the one to adjust. Take a training job—which you're good at—and stay. Prove to Chloe you want her whether you're hanging out here or not."

Gage frowned. "Are you seriously back to that already?"

"Judging by your grumpy face, I'm assuming you'll think about it," East said lightheartedly. "But in the meantime, use what you have to your advantage."

"What do you mean?"

East shrugged. "You want to know Chloe more? Then use what you already know. Get her to break by playing on her weaknesses. It's no secret she has a thing for guys in camo."

Camo? Come to think of it, she *did* give him extra-long glances whenever he was donning his gear…

"Are you saying I should parade myself in front of her like a damn pageant queen?"

"Depends on how badly you want her."

Gage shook his head. East did have a point: Chloe was

no stranger to adjusting the rules of this game to benefit her. Why shouldn't he do the same? He'd use what he had to his advantage.

"Why are you helping me out?" Gage asked.

"Because," East said, "I think you and Chloe are great and terrible for each other. If your plan works, great. If not, you're going to be knocked on your ass, and I'm not going to miss an opportunity to say I told you so when she hands you your nuts."

"Noted," Gage grumbled. But this was the best plan he had at the moment.

"By the way," East said, finally checking his text message. "Our mock victim canceled. He has the flu."

Shit. Gage checked his watch. He had one hour to get into position before the men showed up to start their mission. Where was he going to find a new mock victim on such short—

This was either the best or worst idea he'd had yet.

"I'll take care of the victim," he said. "But we have to get going."

And he was now going to be staying in his camo for longer than he'd thought.

Chloe sighed and walked around the entrance to the state park where Gage had texted her to meet him. All he'd said was: *This is not a dinner date. Wear jeans, tennis shoes, and long sleeves*.

She had half a mind to tell him to take his "non-date" into the mountains and make sure it was never found, but then again, she needed a day off from the stress of preparing the restaurant. What better way to spend it than jean clad and tempting the S&R expert who'd been featured in her fantasies last night?

Hopefully he was finally starting to see reason. The other night, he'd left her wanting more of him. She might have been naked on a table, but he'd cleaned up nicely with his button-up shirt and clean-shaven face. He was hot, and he'd come over ready to take her out. Part of her felt slightly guilty at her deception, but that dwindled when she remembered how well he'd eaten her…dessert.

"Gage?" she called out. The trees to her left rustled, and she spun. Something emerged from the thick canopy of shadows, and she stepped back and gasped.

Gage was in camo pants and a tight green T-shirt, and his face had war paint streaked across it. A massive knife was strapped to his thigh. Complete with a butch black watch and backpack, he looked like GI Joe come to life.

Yes, please.

She liked the way he cleaned up, but honestly, she loved the dirty, dangerous side of him even more. He was all man, muscle, and…

He pulled a small daisy from behind his back and handed it to her with a wink.

Romantic.

Only Gage could pull off the romantic version of Rambo.

She stood frozen. Maybe she should've gotten herself lost in the woods ages ago. Hell, if this guy came to her rescue, she'd play the part of the damsel in distress all day long.

"You look like you're in shock there, sweetheart." He tucked the daisy behind her ear. His fingers lingered a moment by her face, and she leaned into his touch. "I'm equipped to handle people in shock, you know?"

She struggled to stop staring and pause the naughty fantasies involving Gage and his camo. She'd be damned if she fell for whatever he was up to.

"I ah…" She blinked a few times, finally breaking her staring competition with his impressive pecs. "Just admiring the scenery."

"Uh-huh." He flexed his abs enough to call her bullshit. He knew exactly what *scenery* she was admiring.

"What's going on?" she asked, trying to keep her voice normal. But he stepped closer, and those fantasies started to take over again. He looked rough, tough, and a little dirty, but he smelled like pine and spice, and she'd bet her salary he tasted like sweet cinnamon.

"I need you, sweetheart…" He took another step closer. "To be my victim."

She frowned. "What? Is this one of those kinky sex games?" *Because if so, sign me up.*

"You wish." He grinned. "But sadly, no. The team is doing a mock search and rescue. I want you to be my victim."

That's it? He'd called her out here, looking all hot and manly, only to ditch her in the woods? She was hot, bothered, and he'd barely touched her. Now he wanted her to play victim? And not in the cool, sexy way? Eff that.

"No thanks." She crossed her arms. "I'd likely actually get lost and—"

"I'd stay with you the whole time."

That perked her up. "Really?"

They'd be in the woods. Together. She could pull out her best seductress skills and see what he was packing under the camo.

He nodded. "Time is kind of an issue here, so if you're in, I'll take you now."

Please take me now.

Chloe shook off the thought and tried to focus. She didn't have much going on other than burning another attempt at crab cakes and ruining a perfectly good pan, so playing victim wasn't such a bad idea. Especially if there was a chance she could lure him to her side of sex-induced-thinking.

"All right," she said.

And he didn't waste any time. He grabbed her hand and led them through the forest, walking with her for what seemed like forever.

At first, her seduction skills didn't have a chance to work since he was tugging her quickly through the damn old country. She could barely breathe normally, much less speak.

"I thought this was a drill?" she said with a few panting breaths.

But he looked back at her, and damn him, he hadn't even broken a sweat. Fuck cucumbers, Gage was as cool as the air-conditioning she'd left back at her place. Nope, Mr. Army of One was hiking this terrain like it was just another day. Which, for him, it probably was. His boots were steady even when walking on the uneven ground. He obviously knew what he was doing, which made her like him even more.

"It is a drill. But we have to make it count." He glanced back at her and stopped. "Why don't we take a quick break?"

Oh, thank God. She stretched and scanned the area.

"Good girl," Gage said. "You're taking in your surroundings. That's a good sign that you're a survivor."

"Are you reading me now or just offering up lessons on survival?"

"Maybe both. Although, I'd like to think I have a good read on you already." He winked.

She rolled her eyes, but he wasn't wrong. Gage had her number and they both knew it. But this was a chance to dig deeper into his world. And honestly, she wanted to stay in the moment with him, especially since he was in all his sexy gear.

"Well then, why don't you give me a lesson? If we have time, anyway…"

He smiled, but a serious look crossed his face. "There's always time. Let's start by testing your instincts." He pulled out a black bandana from his pocket and tied it around her eyes.

Her world went dark. Gage's breath hit her mouth. She wanted to inhale deeply and bring his mouth to hers, but he kept himself just out of reach.

"I'm going to walk a few yards away, and I want you to use your senses to try to figure out which direction I'm in."

"You said you wouldn't leave me alone," she said quickly.

"I'd never leave you. I'll have eyes on you the whole time. But I want to know if you can figure out a threat."

"You're not a threat," she whispered. But that wasn't totally true—he threatened her sanity and her stance on "casual-only encounters." But she also trusted him so much that she was standing in the middle of God knew where, blindfolded and nodding like an idiot as he walked away from her.

Man…she was either really hard up or delusional. *Or I like him.*

No, definitely not. She was just hard up.

"Imagine you're lost out here. You have to use your senses to survive. Your gut tells you when you're not alone—listen to it. Now count to five, and then when you think you know where I am, take a step toward me."

She nodded, but this felt like more than a standard drill. If she could figure out where Gage was, trust her gut, then move toward him…maybe it'd be a sign that the connection they had was more than casual.

Deep breath.

She couldn't hear him, but Gage had promised he'd stay close. Part of her liked the idea of him watching her. He wouldn't let anything happen to her.

Another deep breath.

He was near—the tingle of his stare prickled her skin. He was right, instincts could tell a lot—and hers were screaming to reach out for Gage.

On a heavy exhale, she took one…two…three steps

toward the direction she thought he was in.

Silence.

Oh no, what if she was wrong? What would it mean? That her gut was lame and was pulling her in the wrong direction? This was stupid. Did she really think she could magically find her way to him in the dark? She should yank off this blindfold and —

"Well done, sweetheart." Gage's voice was thick, laced with pride, and right in front of her. He undid the bandana, and she blinked until he came into focus.

She'd done it. And his lips hovered over hers.

"You should listen to your gut more often. And we should get moving."

He backed off and started walking again.

Gage was messing with her. And the next chance she had to get her hands on him, the claws were coming out. But first she had to catch him, which took a while since she was trailing behind him the rest of their hike.

Finally, after what felt like forever, Gage stopped near a patch of dense trees about fifty yards from the cliffs.

She looked around and inhaled deeply. Sun filtered through the thick trees, lighting the leaves like emeralds swaying around them. The low whistle of underbrush dancing along the ground in the distance added an illusion that felt like real magic.

"I hope I didn't rush you too bad." He handed her his canteen, and she took a few sips. "I wanted to get you out here as quickly as possible."

She handed the water back to him. "Well I got my exercise in for today." Granted, she would have rather burned calories riding Gage's body. Instead, she was stuck in the woods with him looking beyond sexy, but with him acting so professional that she doubted she had a chance in hell of getting him to drop his pants and let her take care of him in the best way she knew how. Her seductress skills didn't stand a chance. Or did they?

She started making her way to the nearby creek.

"Where you going there, sweetheart?"

She glanced over her shoulder. "Just want to enjoy this water over here. Don't worry, I know you've got eyes on me."

And yes he did—his gaze was smoldering, and she had to look away before she got caught up in it. She bent over to run her hands under the clear, chilly water. With wet, cold hands, she gripped the back of her neck and sighed. God that felt good. But her sigh brought a big, rough man her way, and she hid a smile—her seductress skills were working.

"You really should be careful." Gage's raspy voice was directly behind her.

She shifted a bit on the big rocks beneath her feet to look at him. "Why?"

The minute the words came out, she shifted her balance and tilted sideways, jerking toward the creek—

Gage clamped her hip and pulled her toward him. Her heart crashed against her chest, but she couldn't have staged it more perfectly if she'd tried. In less than five minutes she'd gone from across the clearing to pressed against a hard man's muscles and soaking in all of his delicious scent.

"This is uneasy ground you're walking on," Gage said.

"No kidding," she mumbled. Everything about Gage was like feeling her way through something she had no idea how to deal with. And the outdoors weren't helping. She was muddling through her personal life pretty pathetically already—she didn't need the smell of pine and the blister on her toe reminding her how out of her element she was.

She looked into Gage's eyes. She had to take some power back here—being this close to him was awakening that need again. That ache for more.

"Well Mr. Search and Rescue." She ran her hand down

his chest while he held her tightly. "If I were your victim and I slipped and fell, how would you treat me?"

He raised a brow, and a slight grin tugged his face. Oh yeah, he knew what she was going for. And all Chloe could do now was pray he played along.

Please, please play along.

"Well for starters, I'd take you to a secure area." He hoisted her up and walked her over to an area of soft, even ground near a large tree. "Then I'd assess your body."

"I like the sound of that."

"For injury."

Damn it! Pretty soon she'd have such a bad case of "hard-up-itis" she'd start shaking. Or begging. Why did he have to look so hot?

Gage rested his big palms on her shoulders, then slid them up and cupped her neck. The way he angled her head left then right, it was an erotic massage of sorts, and her eyelids were getting heavy.

"Then I'd say, 'How do you feel, ma'am?'"

"Mmm, pretty good," she purred.

He pressed and rubbed his thumbs along the outside of her ears, down her jaw, then back up into her scalp.

"You do feel good," he said lowly. "So no head injury." His hands slipped down to her chest and subtly grazed her breasts. Her nipples perked instantly—she was seriously going to beg any second.

"No head injury," she murmured.

"Any injury in this area?" He rubbed down her sides, feeling her ribs.

He was being professional during their game, but that didn't mean she had to play by the same rules.

"Actually, I'm really aching."

He frowned but waited for her to continue.

"I'm hot." She arched a little further until the U between

his thumb and first finger were right beneath her cleavage. "I'm so hot and so, so achy. Won't you help me with this pain, sir?"

Gage cupped her breasts fully. "Right here?"

She nodded. "Yes, but I can barely feel you. Maybe harder—"

He massaged her breasts slowly, deliberately, until her eyes rolled in the back of her head. His hands on her made her crazy and desperate for more.

Thankfully, she didn't have to ask for more, because he stopped his seductive petting to pinch her nipples.

"Ah! Yes."

"Better, ma'am?" he asked, playing back right along. "I need to make sure you're really okay."

"I appreciate your thoroughness," she breathed. He was so good that she was getting off being felt up. And she didn't give a damn. His hands were magic, and her body was calling out for them.

She couldn't wait. Couldn't hold out anymore. She reached down and gripped his belt.

"How long until they find me?"

"Depends on how good they are, but I took us out a little farther than originally planned, so at least an hour or two."

She looked him over. Her entire body was humming with the need to touch him. Grab on to his strength and revel in it. He was exactly Chloe's type: strong and badass with a heap of attitude and panty-melting swagger. Everything about Gage made her want to give in to the dark need boiling low in her gut.

Time to see how polished her persuasion talents were.

She arched her back even more, pushing her chest into his palms. "What are you going to do with me for a whole hour? In the woods? Alone?" She traced her finger along the fly of his pants.

He slowed, stepped back, and set his pack down. Her heart sank—the connection was gone.

"I thought we could talk."

She groaned and rolled her eyes. "Seriously?"

Gage nodded. He'd lured her out there looking way too hot for his own good, but he was still trying to "get to know her better." This game was becoming a problem—why wouldn't he give in already?

She crossed her arms. "What do I get?"

"What do you want?"

"You."

He smiled. "I want you too, sweetheart."

"Then stop being a brat." She tugged the hem of his shirt. "Can't we do what we always do? Don't you like it? Miss it?"

He cupped the side of her face with one hand and dug his fingers into her hair with the other, then pulled her close until his hard cock pressed against her stomach. "More than you can imagine."

"Then stop with this romance and dating nonsense and just…" She moved to her tiptoes and nipped his bottom lip. "Take me."

"I want *more* of you," he growled against her mouth.

She closed her eyes for a moment. This was backfiring fast. He was supposed to lose his resolve. Instead it was *her* body screaming—no, *begging* for him. Like an addict hit with a bad withdrawal, she was struggling not to give him everything he wanted for one touch.

Get your shit together.

They'd worked out an "even exchange" system the other night. Maybe she could do that again. A little bit for a little bit. Give her body a hit of what she needed so desperately without giving up everything Gage had asked for.

It was worth a shot. Because she was ready to unravel at the seams.

"Fine," she said. "Five minutes of talking, but you have to do it shirtless."

He leaned back. "Seriously?"

"Yep."

She hadn't gotten to really see him in the last few days, and she was dying to stare at him like the eye candy he was. Plus, the more undressed he was, the easier it was to touch him. Maybe take a few licks.

He tugged on his shirt and yanked if off, then tossed it on top of the pack by his feet.

Her jaw slackened. Lord almighty, he was all hard ridges and defined muscles.

"Got what you wanted?" he asked.

She shook her head. "Not even close."

He flexed his abs, and his tan skin rippled like fresh caramel being poured. She wanted to lick him from hips to neck. His low-slung camo pants complete with belt and tactical gear were enough to send her into cardiac arrest on the off chance he'd administer mouth-to-mouth.

How the hell did he affect her like this? No other man ever made her swoon at the sight of him. But Gage's presence alone had her squeezing her thighs together because one look, one move toward her, and she—

"What has you biting your lip so hard, sweetheart?"

"Thinking of sinking my teeth into you," she answered honestly. Though the words were true, her mind was in a daze. He was all she could focus on, like he'd hypnotized her. "It's embarrassing, really."

"How?" he asked.

"Because I know how you move." She lifted her chin at his arms. "Your shoulders have shifted, and your hands flexed like you're ready to scoop me up and own every inch of me."

"That right?" he whispered, stepping toward her.

She nodded. "I've felt it. And I want it so bad. I respond

before you do anything, because the anticipation is the worst." Their eyes met. "I know what I'm missing, and I kind of hate you for it."

He nodded. "I feel the same way."

She tilted her head. "What do you mean?"

"I've caught glimpses of you, and I want more. Don't think just because I want to know *you* that I have any less hunger for…" His gaze ran over her body. "It's taking everything I have not to let you put those teeth on me right now. You're almost too much for me."

"Yeah, almost too much. But clearly not tempting enough, otherwise you'd—"

"Give in?" he asked. "Don't test me, because I fucking want to. But to get what I'm after, I have to stick to my mission."

Chloe scowled. "Why can't you fuck me and be happy?"

"Because," he snapped, "every time I see you, it's better than the last. Because like it or not, I *am* getting to know you and reading you better. And the kind of passion, the moans and screams and claws you have, keep me hard weeks after I see you. And it just. Gets. Better. I'll chase that desire all damn day if I get more of you." He took another step. "Is it hard to believe I could actually like you, Chloe? Want to be with you for sex *and* you?"

She bit her lip again. Truth was, she *didn't* believe it, and even if she did, she wouldn't give in. Being the hot piece Gage nailed whenever he came into town had clear lines. She knew where she stood, and there wasn't a chance of getting caught up and hurt because she'd complicated their arrangement with feelings.

This had to stay a casual sexual relationship because she couldn't risk there being a day when Gage might not want to come back ever again. Her mother had given in to that kind of relationship, and it had ruined her until the day she'd died.

She'd pined for Chloe's father, like she was so lost without him that she couldn't accept he was never coming back.

Chloe would never let herself open her heart to a man when it meant he could leave her, too, the same way her father had left her mother.

The sex-only relationship she had with Gage was safe. This way she could savor him and let him go each time with no expectations, always ready for the possibility that he would never come back.

She ran her palm up his stomach, slowly taking in every nook and ridge of hardness. He relaxed his shoulders on a sharp exhale. Gage was right, chasing the kind of passion they had was a heady thing. And she'd chase, too, because she wasn't ready to give up the intensity they shared. She could fake a little romance without getting in too deep if it meant more of him.

"We talked." She skimmed her fingertips down his stomach, to the edge of his waistband. His pants were tented by an erection he wasn't even trying to hide. She hovered closer, pressing her mouth against his chest as her fingers dipped to the knuckle into his pants.

His breath was ragged, his skin heated. He was fighting himself. Hopefully he'd see reason and finally give in.

"Give me one thing," he said. "One honest, true, real thing about yourself."

She met his gaze and paused. "I can't cook. I own my mother's restaurant and can't cook."

She was entrusted to run her mother's legacy and was failing. Reintroducing her mom's food to the menu and renovating the balcony didn't make Chloe competent. And that realization was one she struggled with every day.

"I'm sure that's not true," he offered. He was trying to be sweet, and she appreciated that, but...

"Nope, it's true. And normally I wouldn't mind so much,

but there's just one thing—" She stopped herself from going into details, because it was those details that made it hard to swallow the failure rising in her throat.

"What one thing, sweetheart?" he pressed. "You want to cook something special?"

She was playing a dangerous game with a man that she knew better than to play with at all. Their one rule, "casual," had kept her safe every time he'd come and every time he'd left. But now he'd changed the rules. Now he wanted "romance." Now he wanted her to open up to him. Now he wanted her to feel for him with her heart, not just her body.

"Forget it," she said.

"No." His voice was blunt and deep. Not harsh, but that one word was said with such authority that Chloe registered the intent. He was telling her he would not forget a thing.

"I want to make something specific for the restaurant anniversary coming up, but I'm struggling. Happy now?" she said with her own snap. She didn't want to go into her shortcomings. Didn't want to discuss "real" things, like how she missed her mother and how she hated the loss of her. Hated how her mother had lived her last several years with a broken heart because she was waiting on a man. Hated that deep down, Chloe feared she was looking at the man who could ruin her the same way.

She shook her head. No way in hell would she think about this, much less tell Gage about it. Time for the sex. Not the reality.

"Now can we get back to this…" She reached into his pants a little further.

"Chloe…"

"I'm right here." She placed another soft kiss over his nipple. "The question is, what are you going to do about it?" She bit down on his meaty pec, and he growled and drove his hands into her hair. He pressed her against the nearest tree and kicked her legs apart.

Chloe smiled, and the low hum of need she'd been fighting burst into overdrive. She was done with reality. Done with talking. Now it was time for what they did best.

She clawed at his hips, pulled him close between her spread legs, and rocked on his hard cock, hitting the perfect spot. Even between their pants, he knew how to move, where to touch, how to turn her on.

He kissed her hard as the grip on her hair tightened further. He pulled—and she gasped. The shock of pain and pleasure always hit her like a surprise, and she loved it. Gage didn't wait. Didn't negotiate. He took her exactly how she liked it.

"You drive me crazy." He bit her tongue. "So fucking crazy I want to remind you who's in charge."

"Yes, do it!" She grinded her hips against him. She was wild for him. Desperate. He looked like her personal Army of One, and she needed him.

Her eyes snapped open. She looked him over—a wall of muscle, glory, camo, *and* the face paint? He was rugged and "her type" to the Nth degree of hotness.

"You did this on purpose." She shoved at his chest, but he gathered her wrists and locked them behind her, wedging them between the tree trunk and her back.

"You dressed like this on purpose. Tried to get me to give in to you," she said.

With his free hand, he unbuttoned her jeans and tugged them down. Once they bunched around her thighs, he pushed them to the ground with his foot, then locked her legs at her ankles. With his weight on her pants, the bunched cloth acted like cuffs. She was standing, legs spread, and couldn't move.

"Just because I happen to look like your own personal fantasy, doesn't mean you should hold it against me," he said. "Besides, isn't this what you wanted?" He unfastened his pants.

Yes, but he'd made her give up a real detail about herself. "I want you. But you…you're…"

"Not playing fair?" he finished.

He reached into his pants, gripped his cock, and ran the head along her folds. She groaned. "Kind of like that little stunt you pulled the other night with your 'quick meal'?"

He had her there. She might have used that to her advantage, like Gage was using his camo and manliness to his. And she was melting for him.

"Please take me now," she begged as the hot crown of his cock barely nudged her opening. She lifted her hips to try to take him into her body, but he stilled her.

"We haven't had a dinner date yet. And fucking in the woods doesn't count as romance."

Her eyes met his. "Then what…"

He thrust hard against her, running his big rod along her sex, and her head fell back. Her legs and hands were pinned. His big palm pressed against her stomach to keep her from moving. He had her in every way. And he wasn't going to take all of it.

The thought sent fire raging through her; a cocktail of frustration mixed with lust and pent-up need.

"Feels like a compromise," he said. The way he worked his hips was out of some manual for *How to Be a Sex God without Actually Having Sex*.

The velvety head of his cock briefly prodded at her opening, then ran up and down between her folds, hitting every nerve ending. He pumped faster against her clit before sliding back down to her opening, but never breaching.

He was spreading her moisture, using nothing but his impressive cock, and she was on the brink of coming from him *not* fucking her.

"You're evil," she said, but when he thrust up, pressing

hard against her clit and rubbing wildly, she lost her voice.

"Really? Because it sounds like you're enjoying this. Perhaps a *thank you* is more in line."

"Thank you," she whispered. "Thank you. Please…" She tried to wiggle and get more, but it was no use.

"Please what?"

"Keep doing this. I want to come so bad."

"I want you to," he rasped in her ear. "Because you're going to make me come, too."

He yanked up her shirt, exposing her stomach, and moved faster. "Do you have any idea what you do to me? Making me crazed with needing to be inside you, and you're going to make me come without even getting the chance."

She knew the feeling. He had more restraint than she did, because she was ready to hand over anything he wanted if he'd take her deep.

The fire in her veins boiled and climbed from her toes to her breasts, snapping flicks of pleasure along the way. Her orgasm swept her up, took her over, and she couldn't breathe. Didn't want to. Didn't need to. Because Gage was right there to breathe for her. Catch her. Consume her.

He groaned low, and the hot lash of his release hit her stomach as he moved up and down. After several deep breaths, his hold on her loosened. They both looked at his seed marking her. He smiled like he'd won some victory, and truth was, he kind of had. Gage exercised control in a way she'd never seen—and now she was marked by him.

He kissed her once, tucked his cock back into his pants, then reached in his pack and grabbed a wet wipe. He cleaned her stomach, then pulled her pants up and fastened them.

"I'll be honest, sweetheart. This is the best mock rescue to date."

She took a deep breath, trying not to let frustration override the bliss. But Gage was winning. She was ready to give in to whatever he wanted if it meant she got to have him.

Stay. Strong.

Be the fantasy. Not the reality.

"Well," she said casually and picked a piece of bark off of her shoulder. "If half of your team responds the way you do, they should be here in no time."

His eyes turned dark as he warded off a snarl. She was being bratty, but she didn't care. He was messing with her sexy time and holding his body hostage against her.

She needed to make him break, and fast—before she broke first.

He was back against her in a millisecond. His big body pressed hard against her front and the tree against her back.

He cupped her face, and his fierce gaze was so wild and desperate, she couldn't tell if he was mad or terrified.

"This is the last time." He kissed her bottom lip. "The last opportunity." Kiss. "Chloe, will you have dinner with me?"

She leaned back enough to meet his eyes once more. Gage McGraw, the man who issued orders and expected to have them followed, just *asked* her.

All the venom she'd built up, the wily exchange of wills, all fell between them. The only thing left was Gage gazing at her like he really saw her. And she couldn't deny him.

"Please."

That was her undoing.

"Okay," she whispered.

A huge smile split his face, and he kissed her. Once hard and fast, the next soft, then small, light brushes of his lips, until finally he took her mouth completely.

"I promise romance isn't as bad as you think," he said.

Chloe somehow doubted it. Especially because she had no idea what she was doing. But she was sure of two things. One, she was getting in way over her head. Two, she wouldn't be able to stop herself.

Chapter Five

Gage's phone pinged with a text message from Chloe.

What's your favorite dessert?

He stopped rolling the cuffs on his blue button-up and responded easily with the truth.

You.

Funnily enough, he was a bit nervous. While part of him had been confident he could eventually get Chloe to cave and go on a date with him, another part of him thought it'd never happen. But it *was* happening. Tonight.

After their little escapade in the woods, he'd replayed in his mind over and over the one word she'd said when he'd asked her again for just one date.

Okay.

She'd said *okay.* Now it was his shot to show her how much more they could be. And why he wanted to keep coming back to this town and to her.

His phone pinged again.

*By the way, don't worry about picking me up. I'll meet
you at the restaurant.*

He almost protested, because walking to her door and
getting her was part of the date. Granted, he'd never been
strictly traditional, but with Chloe, he wanted to do things
right—take her hand as she got out of the car, open the
restaurant door for her, pull her seat out. But he was walking
on thin ice with a date in the first place, and he didn't want to
push his luck. If she wanted to meet him at the restaurant, he
wouldn't push the issue.

Assuming this wasn't some elaborate ruse.

*If you stand me up, sweetheart, we're going to have
words.*

A few seconds passed, and then she wrote back.

Please, God, no more talking.

He chuckled while responding.

Yep. Don't think I don't know how to punish you.

Her response came within seconds: *You wouldn't dare.*
Gage grinned from ear to ear as he typed out his reply.

*I'll talk to you all night. Then again in the morning. I'll
talk to you so hard and so much you won't be able to
handle another conversation for weeks.*

And send.

He called to double-check the reservation he'd made
at Le Coeur's—a fancy French restaurant in town. At first,
Chloe had asked why she'd eat somewhere other than her

own restaurant, but she'd seemed to melt with relief when he'd suggested that maybe she needed a night off from everything.

He thanked the hostess for confirming his reservation, then hung up and saw he had another text from Chloe.

> *Your threat is noted, and I believe you. I'm showing up tonight so we can finally get down to the good stuff. But I swear to God, if I buy you surf and turf and you don't put out at the end of the evening, then I'll be the one having words with you.*

He laughed again. God, he liked her. So much. She was funny, strong-willed, and so damn sexy it made his head spin. Their little game was reversed in a lot of ways, but when it came down to it, they both played their part well. And his part was to keep a hold of Chloe and pleasure her until she couldn't entertain the idea of anything—or anyone—else.

> *I see we understand each other then. See you soon, sweetheart.*

His phone pinged once more.
Yes, you will.

Chloe had no idea what she was doing. It'd taken her all day and more research than she'd care to admit to prepare for tonight's date. The cute little restaurant was on the waterfront, and Gage sat at a table nestled in the corner with a single candle in the middle. She hadn't meant to be late, but she was.

Now he probably thought she was standing him up. Well, maybe that'd make him all the more eager when she finally went over. Assuming he didn't walk out.

She shook her head and banished the thought. He

wouldn't walk out. And she shouldn't care if he did.

She stood near the bar and watched the strong, capable search and rescuer sitting alone. Waiting for her.

She'd give him what he wanted just this once. This one night, one date, one act of romance, she could handle that much. At least, that was the pep talk she'd been dishing to herself since the almost sex they'd had in the woods.

He'd asked her questions as though he really did want to know her more. Know about her mother. Her past. And that scared her. Because deep down, she wanted to open up to him. She trusted him. Which was why she'd shown up at all tonight. But if she thought too long about it, she might back out.

Instead, she took a step forward.

She adjusted her purse—which felt heavier than normal—and then smoothed one hand down her dress and walked to her…date.

When he caught her walking toward him, those incredible eyes of his lit up. A man looking at her like that did weird things to her chest. Then again, it wasn't *any* man who could do this to her with a look; only the man she wanted.

Heat rushed to her cheeks, and she suppressed a nervous giggle.

Gage stood, walked around the table, and pulled her chair out for her. "You look beautiful."

Oh, he was good. His simple gesture and smooth words coated her skin like rich honey.

"So do you." She took in his pressed shirt and black pants. He smelled like leather, spice, and all man—she could get lost in his scent.

"Before I sit, I have some stuff for you," she said.

Gage raised a brow as she fished through her purse.

"Here." She handed him a mini bouquet of roses. Actually, now that she looked at the semi-smooshed flowers, maybe it hadn't been the wisest idea to carry them in her purse.

He laughed and took them anyway. "Nice touch."

She handed him a note. "And this is for you, too."

He unfolded it. His soothing laugh came back, and her face warmed.

"You're hot?" he asked, reading the two words she'd scribbled on the paper.

"It's true." She shrugged. "And here's one more thing." She grabbed the last present and handed it to him.

"Edible panties?" He grinned at the packaged strawberry thong. "I like where your mind is at, sweetheart, but I don't think these will fit me."

"These are romantic," she declared proudly. "I Googled it."

He took a step closer, and his smile turned into something more serious. "What do you mean?"

She shrugged, trying really hard not to feel like an idiot. But tonight was important to him, and she was actually trying. Even if, judging by his reaction, she was doing pretty terribly. Nothing to do but admit how much she was lacking in this department.

"I read up on romance." She stared at her feet. "The top romantic suggestions included surprise your date with flowers…" She glanced at the ceiling, concentrating on recalling every pointer from the website. "Write your date a sweet note."

Granted, all she'd come up with was *You're hot*, but she was still a novice at the romance stuff.

He took a step closer and cupped her hip, silently asking her to go on.

She finally met his gaze. "And prepare your date's favorite dessert."

"That's why you asked earlier?" he said.

She nodded. "And since you said your favorite dessert

was me…" She leaned in a little, and the wrapper of the edible panties crinkled a bit in his tight grip.

"You're very clever. And I love all of it." He gently kissed her lips, soft but thorough, stealing her breath and thoughts.

This was so out of her element. "You don't think it's stupid?" She wasn't good with romance, but she wanted to make Gage feel all the things he made her feel. Wanted. Special. Seen.

"You're incredible, sweetheart," he whispered against her lips. "Thank you."

Chloe smiled—she'd won a small victory here. Maybe he was right. Maybe this romance thing wasn't so bad. Granted, she'd given her date a fruit-flavored thong in the middle of a five star restaurant, but whatever.

She gave him a final kiss, then took her seat. Gage set his gifts on the edge of the table and sat, too.

Across the white linen and flickering candle, his eyes sparkled. Looking at this man made her melt. Just being across from him was its own delicious kind of foreplay hinting at what the night would bring when they finally made it to the bedroom. Why hadn't she agreed to this sooner?

Oh, right. Because she was feeling something for him. A lot of something.

But she wouldn't get caught up in those thoughts and fears. Not with so much riding on tonight.

Tonight, she wouldn't overthink it. She'd just enjoy dinner. And later, she'd enjoy him.

"Five star restaurant and we cut out for ice cream?" Chloe said, walking along Main Street, licking her vanilla ice cream cone. Vanilla. Not chocolate. As far as Gage could figure, her choice indicated she was neither sad nor stressed. Excellent.

He also knew the creamery was her favorite. Every time they'd talked in the past, she'd brought up the flavor she'd tried that week.

"Thought you'd like my dessert choice." He took a lick of his own strawberry cone.

Her eyes met his. "I do. Very much."

Gage had never expected tonight to go as well as it did. Dinner was wonderful, but Chloe was even better. She was trying, which meant she clearly cared about him—that alone was enough to make him hold on to the hope they could actually make this work.

They walked down the street, the lights of the nearby shops twinkling. She slipped her free hand into his, and it felt good. Better than good. It felt right. As though strolling down the street after a nice night of talking and laughing was so normal, he could feel it in his bones.

And he wanted more. Wanted to know her more. Wanted her to finish all the things she'd ever stopped herself from telling him. Wanted to hear her mind when she spoke and watch her eyes when she laughed. He just wanted…more.

"Ever think about adding ice cream to the menu at your restaurant?" he asked.

She smiled and took another lick of her cone. "Are you kidding? I could never beat the creamery." She moaned around another long lick of the ice cream, and the sight of her tongue made Gage's cock take notice. But he stuck to his mission. Getting to spend time with her outside of bed. If this worked, it would be all the more satisfying when they fully gave in to their desire.

"Besides," she finished, "Natalie would kill me if I had a direct dessert competition."

He nodded. Time to push just a little bit. "So it's safe to say that the dish you're trying to make for the anniversary isn't a sweet one?"

Her stride slowed and she glanced at the ground. Gage knew that look. Like if she could turn her vanilla cone into chocolate right now, she just might. But when she looked at him, there was a different light sparkling behind her eyes. Like she…trusted him. At least wanted to see if she could.

"I'm trying to make crab cakes. My mother's epic, amazing, can't-be-replicated-ever crab cakes."

"I see," he said. And he wanted to help. Because of all the times he'd seen Chloe, he'd never seen something be so important to her. "There are only so many ingredients in crab cakes. Did your mom get creative and use a difficult recipe?"

"No," she said calmly. "That's just it. It's not putting them together that's hard, it's how she cooked them. The ingredients I can handle, well…for the most part. But no matter what I do, I can't cook them right. It's really annoying."

She huffed and took another lick of her cone. But she kept holding his hand. Kept talking to him. And damn, Gage wanted to keep that rhythm going. She was opening up. Trusting him with more.

"I always end up burning them. Even when I turn the stove down." She shook her head. "I swear the stove just hates me. It's secretly a robot out to destroy anything I bring near it."

"That's a valid hypothesis," he said.

She laughed and nudged him. "Yeah, evil robot stove is way more plausible than me not being able to boil water."

"Surely you can boil water…" he said with a wink. "Just don't go too crazy and put an egg in it or anything."

"Oh God no!" she teased. "My luck, the damn egg would turn into a chicken, flip me off, and fly out of the pot."

"Now you sound magical."

"Not in the kitchen, I'm afraid. Which is hard, because my mom was so good in there. Like second nature. I can still remember how it smelled with her in it. Like she could create anything. There was always this smell of...love." She didn't make a sound, but her grip on his hand tightened, and Gage waited a breath and silently begged for her to continue. Finally, she said, "Sounds stupid, doesn't it? The smell of love."

"Not at all," Gage said. "It's how you know her. How you remember her. It's comforting."

She stared at him. "It really is. The clicking sound right before the burner lights or the soft sway of a kettle before it whistles are like triggers. For a second, I can almost see her. Forget that she's gone. And it's in that tiny moment, I have her back."

Gage squeezed her hand. "It's like she's still with you."

The corner of her mouth trembled. Just barely, but he couldn't miss it.

"But those moments are getting shorter and shorter and fewer and further between."

"You miss her," he said.

"Yes. So much. Even when she was alive I missed her."

That made him frown. "What do you mean?"

She shook off that last question, and with one last lick of her cone, she dropped the rest into the trash can as they approached her restaurant. Gage did the same thing and walked her toward the entrance of her place.

Their talking time was over. He could sense it. He wanted to know more. Wanted her to dive deeper, but he would take what he could get. Besides, she'd already given him quite a bit tonight. He was grateful for that small step.

"Well, this is me," she said as they rounded the restaurant to her door around the back of the building.

"Nice place," he said, falling into the role of her new date. A role he was liking. "I hear this is a pretty special restaurant."

"It is..." She glanced away, as if mulling something over. Then she turned back to him and said, "The twentieth anniversary of this restaurant is happening next weekend. You should come. If you want."

Holy hell, Chloe was inviting him to the anniversary event? That was an invitation not just to a date. That was an invitation into her world.

Hope spread from his chest to every other part of him. He'd brought her into the great outdoors and she'd passed with flying colors—not that he'd been grading her. But she was an A+ no matter what. Now maybe their worlds could merge—or at least, maybe they could step in and out of each other's worlds with minimal issues.

"I'll be there," he promised.

She smiled and swayed, playing coy, and his body went on alert.

"I sure had a lovely time, Mr. McGraw." She batted those long lashes, playing the cute and not-so-subtle role.

Now he would play, too.

"I had a mighty fine time myself, ma'am." It went against his New York accent to drop his vowels and coat his words with the North Carolina twang, but it made Chloe smile.

"Would you like to come up for a cup of coffee?" she asked sweetly and leaned in. "And by coffee, I mean sex."

He grinned. "Absolutely."

She rushed up the stairs. Gage didn't get two feet into her apartment before she slammed the front door and plastered him against it.

Nothing ever felt as good as Chloe wanting him.

"Anxious?" he said between bites at her lips and deep tongue thrusts into her mouth.

She drove her hands into his hair and tugged him closer. "You have no idea."

"Oh, I think I do." He scooped her up, and her legs locked around his waist as he carried her to the couch. With her wrapped around him, he sat and let her straddle him. She wasted no time tugging on his shirt, freeing the buttons, and trailing her hot mouth down his chest.

"Jesus, you feel amazing." He reached up beneath her dress, grabbed her ass, and groaned. "No panties?"

"They get in the way."

"All damn night you were walking around without panties on?" he growled.

"Yep." She rocked against his jean-clad cock. "Now what are you going to do about it?"

And wasn't that the question of their entire relationship? He ground her against him, and her breath hitched against his chest. She bit down on his pec and reached between them to unfasten his belt.

"Now," she said. "I can't wait anymore."

"Whatever you want." She'd fulfilled his request for romance and the date, now he'd more than meet every desire she had. Time to remind her exactly what he was good at— pleasuring her.

He unzipped the back of her dress as she unzipped his jeans. The material covering her plump breasts fell down her flat stomach and pooled at her waist. With one arm wrapped around her lower back, he palmed the perfect handful of her breast and sucked hard.

"Yes, please, more," she cried to the ceiling. He gently bit the tip of her nipple and pulled her closer until her wet heat pressed against the throbbing crown of his shaft. He scooted enough to peel his jeans down his thighs, finally baring his entire length.

So close. They'd been skin on skin a few times now this visit, the chance for him to again be inside her, and he'd resisted every time after he'd first seen her at the bar.

Except tonight would be different. Tonight, he was taking everything. No more playing. No more games. He'd bury himself inside her until neither of them could move.

"Do you have any idea what you do to me?" He sucked her other breast.

"I'm concentrating on what you're doing to me." She arched her back, offering up more sweet skin.

"I'm going to be doing a lot more to you here in a minute."

She palmed his jeans. His cock was hard and pulsing, and the brief touches of her damp flesh against it were driving him fucking insane.

No more waiting.

Not tonight.

She finally found the condom in his pocket she'd been looking for. She pulled it out, ripped it open, and worked it over his cock. Her arms pushed her breasts together like the best damn offering he'd ever been presented with. He buried his face in her soft cleavage, sucking, kissing, and licking. Back and forth, he took one nipple into his mouth, then the other. Devouring her in long draws and coming back for more.

When she'd covered his cock with the condom, she wiggled and tried to get closer, but he cupped her ribs and lifted her until her hot flesh was right above his waiting cock.

She gripped his shoulders, looked him in the eye, and whispered, "Please."

It was all he needed to hear. He set her down on him, impaling her as he went.

They gasped together. She was tight, hot, drenched, and it was all for him. All the pent-up need of the past few days, hell, the past few *months*, were finally culminating in this single moment.

"More," she begged, clawing at him. One word with so much meaning: deeper, harder.

Gage wanted more, too. He sat forward on the couch and tugged her knees until she was wrapped around him.

He thrust deep. "Like that, sweetheart?" She nodded vigorously while grinding her hips against him. No up and down, that'd be too much space. He was sheathed to the hilt and wasn't fucking going anywhere. He stayed deep, rocking enough to hit her every inner inch while she worked him right back.

Grinding and moving. So damn close he could feel her everywhere.

"Missed you. Missed this," she said.

"Me too," he rasped. He reached between their bodies and spread her sex with two fingers so that her clit rubbed against his lower stomach.

"Oh, God, so good," she moaned. As she whipped her hips in his lap and he delivered deep thrust after thrust, her slick little bundle of nerves glided along his abs, and with every sweep, her channel gripped him tighter.

"Lean back." He cupped her waist and held her steady as she obeyed. Her back arched, breasts high and round, those pink nipples pointing to the sky, and her long hair danced around his shins.

She was at his mercy. His. And he had a front row view of her sexy body spread out and at his disposal. She trusted him to hold her, and that was a gift he wanted to take. He'd hold on to her now and every time he returned. He'd keep her safe.

"Hold on," he growled. With a tight grip on her, he leaned forward, never breaking their connection, and laid her on the floor, following her down. "I'm just getting started with you."

Her legs locked tighter around him as he thrust into her, over and over, each time harder and deeper than the last.

"Yes! Oh please, please baby." She'd never used an endearment with him before—it was like a shot of sugar to his veins. He reached beneath her, grabbed her shoulders, and pulled down as he plunged up. He was being rough, but he couldn't stop. He needed to feel her everywhere.

Good thing she didn't want him to stop.

Her fingernails scoured down his back. "Right there!"

He growled, loving the sting. The raw, wild passion. It was all Chloe. All he thought of when he was away from her. All he wanted when he was near her.

He fucked her impossibly hard, and she was there to take it all. When her tight sheath clamped down on him, her body tensed and gifted him with her release.

"That's it, sweetheart," he whispered in her ear as she let herself go. "Show me how much you missed this. How much you want it."

She moaned and pulled at him. Writhing, shivering, begging. She was gone—spiraling into a powerful orgasm he was proud to have given her. And he was there to cover her. Catch her. And go with her.

His balls were heavy, and he couldn't resist anymore. With her name in his throat, he pumped in and out while he shook with his release.

Slickened with sweat and breathing against him, she cupped his face and kissed him wildly. His cheeks, his chin, his nose. Rained down praise and satisfaction without saying a word. It was these moments he felt immortal. Nothing could touch him so long as he had her praise. As long as she wanted him.

Yet one word kept beating in the back of his brain…

More.

Chapter Six

Chloe dropped in some change, opened the newspaper bin, and grabbed a fresh copy. After the other night with Gage, it was difficult to think of anything but him. Or his body. Or the way he owned hers.

But she had a restaurant to run and an event around the corner.

She opened the newspaper on the side of a busy street and skimmed through it.

"Damn it," she huffed, taking apart the newspaper and reading the social section another time to make sure she hadn't missed the article on her restaurant.

"What are you doing?" Michelle Ruby asked, stepping out of her boutique. The fashionable city woman owned and ran Chic Storm, and judging by the few looky-loos hovering around the storefront display, the boutique was doing well today.

Which wasn't surprising. Even though Michelle was relatively new to town, her high-end fashion apparel was already a staple around Beaufort.

"Just checking the paper." Chloe crumpled it back together. The sun was already burning off the morning dew and making way for a bright summer day, yet a gray cloud hovered right above her head.

Michelle looked at the paper. "Are you job hunting or something?" Her bright red hair was fastened into a bun, and her light blue eyes were lined with smoky kohl that made her look like a Paris model.

"No, I'm looking for something. The paper was supposed to do a little article about my restaurant." And her mother. "It was supposed to come out last week, but I still haven't seen it."

Last week. As in exactly five days ago. Chloe had been so excited and had gotten up at dawn to get the paper, but the article hadn't been there. She'd checked every day since, even the online version, but had seen nothing.

Silly thing was, it was important to her. Yes, the article would help advertise the anniversary, but it was more than that. The piece was about her mother, how she'd opened the bar with little more than a dream and a small business loan. Twenty years later, it was the center point of the town. And it was struggling. Chloe was determined to bring back the joy and light that made the restaurant great, including her mother's food. Just the possibility of this article gave her a flare of connection to her mother. Like others could still experience her memory.

"Oh, I saw that!" Michelle said. "It was an insert a few days ago."

"An insert?"

She nodded. "Yeah, like a little two page spread. Had some pictures and a story about the bar and its origins. The woman who opened it was really incredible. She renovated her house into a restaurant!"

Chloe nodded. "Yeah, I know. She was my mother."

Michelle gasped. "Oh, I'm sorry." She clasped her hands together. "I should have put that together. Let me go check to see if I saved the insert."

"Thanks, I appreciate it."

She nodded and hustled into her boutique while Chloe gripped the paper tighter. She already knew what Michelle would say when she came back. It was an insert, which meant she'd thrown it away. Chloe knew Michelle had done that because *Chloe* had done that. The inserts in the paper were usually a bunch of ads and the local grocery store deals of the week. She hadn't thought the article would be amongst the filler.

"Beautiful day," a smooth sexy voice said near her.

"Are you stalking me?" she said to Gage as he stepped in front of her.

"I'm trained to search and rescue people," he said.

"So is that a yes?"

He glanced at Michelle's shop, then back at Chloe. Maybe he was trying to get another look at Michelle? Not that Chloe cared or anything. They weren't committed—far from it. One date didn't mean anything, and one night of hot sex didn't mean anything either.

Yep…totally didn't care.

Gage smiled. "I won't admit to stalking off the clock. But I must say that a beautiful woman puts even a beautiful day to shame."

Chloe glanced at where Michelle had disappeared to. "Yeah, we all know how beautiful Michelle is."

She wasn't jealous he was talking about another woman. No reason for her to care.

He tucked a lock of hair behind Chloe's ear. "I was commenting on the beautiful woman in front of me."

"Smooth."

"Hey, that was one of my best lines." He winked at her,

and that mushy feeling flared up in the way only he could manage. She laughed a little. But when he flashed those dimples, he had her hooked.

Oh God…were they flirting?

Not the sexy *I want in your pants* flirting, but the cutesy *Will you take me to the sock hop?* flirting. It needed to stop. Now.

"So what are you doing?" he asked.

"I was heading to work, just stopping to get the paper." She tapped the small bin where the *Beaufort Daily Gazette* rested.

He opened his mouth, but Michelle's voice boomed out, followed by the clicking of her four-inch stilettos.

"I'm so sorry, Chloe, I don't have it. I even checked my recycling, but it was picked up yesterday. I would have saved it if I'd known."

Chloe tried not to let the hollow feeling creep in. If it had run a few days ago, all the papers were gone by now. "Totally fine," she said. "I appreciate you looking."

"Looking for what?" Gage asked.

"There was an article about Chloe's mom and her restaurant in the paper," Michelle said.

At the same time, Chloe shot out, "Nothing."

He glanced between them. Chloe wasn't interested in standing around. Her eyes stung, and Gage, with his big shoulders and muscly arms, looked too huggable for her to stay. Especially since she needed a hug then. The exact kind of need she couldn't allow herself to feel.

"Bye," she said quickly and hustled off. The bar was the beacon at the end of the street, and she was almost there. She had to toughen up. Certain things couldn't be changed: her mother was gone, her father had long ago disappeared, and she'd missed the paper she was dying to see.

This was why she tried not to care about things…because

disappointment usually followed.

"You're rocking one sour look." Natalie sipped her milkshake at the bar as the night wound down. "This is delicious. Maybe you should make yourself one to cheer you up."

"It's an adult twist on a s'mores milkshake. Marshmallow vodka," Chloe said. She couldn't cook for shit, but she could make some awesome drinks.

"So, so good." Natalie slurped up the last of it through her straw. "But seriously, what's going on? You've been mopey all day."

"Just a lot on my mind." Like the article. Like Gage. The more she thought about him, the more she wished she didn't, because it was consuming. She'd waited for him to show up tonight…and he hadn't. Of course, she hadn't invited him to come to the bar. And he hadn't said he would. Yet here she was waiting for him.

She felt like she had rocks on her chest—God, she was worse than a teen waiting for her crush to call.

Why had she gone out with him? She should have stuck to sex, but no, he'd insisted and she'd given in to the date and romance. And now she was pining.

"I hate this feeling," she whispered. Hope was a dangerous thing, and so was wanting too much. Chloe had learned early on that people always leave, so it was best not to get attached. Yet right now, the one guy pursuing her was doing what she wanted—staying away. And it hurt anyway.

Truth was, she didn't want him to stay away—but she didn't want him too close.

"You thinking about the hottie in camo?" Natalie said.

"Kind of."

Natalie smiled. "Sometimes admitting what you want isn't so bad."

"It's more complicated than that."

"Yeah, he wants to spend time with you out of the sack, only to get you back in the sack when you're done. Isn't that all...good?"

"You'd think so." But it wasn't. Not for Chloe. She wanted to maintain some level of indifference—it was safer, even if she had to fake it. Being the fantasy and a little unobtainable kept people interested longer. And she wanted Gage to stay interested. But if it became too real, all their *stuff* would come out—emotions. The kind that came with claws and wanted to attach to things.

"What would be so bad?" Natalie said. "You may like him."

"I do like him," Chloe countered. "That's not the problem."

"Oh, I see. You don't want to like him too much."

Chloe nodded. "Something like that." It was the first time she'd admitted it out loud.

"Ladies."

Chloe's heart leaped out of her chest as she turned and saw the owner of the voice. Gage. He was here—he'd come after all. And the only thing that matched her happiness at him showing up was realizing how sad she would have felt if he hadn't.

Gage walked up to the bar with a small box under his arm.

"You really *are* stalking me," she said, trying for mock irritation.

"Hard to call it stalking when everyone knows you work here. Not exactly detective work, sweetheart." He dropped the box on the counter.

Natalie hopped up and winked at Chloe as she scurried to the bathroom. Her friend wasn't exactly subtle.

"What's in the box?" she asked Gage.

He rested an arm over the top. "It's for you."

"If it's a severed head I'm going to be pissed."

He grinned. "Nah, nothing so dramatic. Why don't you open it and see?"

She hesitated, lifted the lid, and—

"How…what…how?" Chloe glanced between him and the box. She reached in and grabbed the stack of inserts from the newspaper. At least twenty copies of the anniversary article.

"This has been out of print for at least a few days…" She couldn't believe it—not only did she have more copies than she'd ever need, but the papers were brand new. A stack of starched, pressed, crisp inserts. How?

Gage shrugged. "Had a chat with the head of the paper."

Her eyes widened. "What, you walked in and—"

"It took some persuading, but this is what you wanted, right?"

She looked at the stack. He hadn't just found her a copy. He'd found her twenty.

"Yes," she whispered. After everything, Gage had come in and saved the day.

And that reality hit a spot between her ribs that made her heart soften for him.

He ran a hand along the back of his neck. "I thought maybe some extras would be smart, so you could give them out or scrapbook them or something…"

Was Gage actually…nervous? Like he was worried about whether *she* would be happy with his gift. The need to hug him came flooding back double time. Not to mention—he thought she scrapbooked? Adorable.

"Thank you." She ran her palm over the stack again. "This is really amazing."

He shrugged but leveled his intense gaze on her. "It's my

job to find things, sweetheart. Making you happy is a bonus."
He patted the counter and turned to leave.

"Gage?"

He glanced back.

Chloe bit her lip. She could do this. Deep breaths. "Would you, um, want to have dinner with me tomorrow night?"

Gage's eyes widened and his eyebrows arched. "Are you asking me on a date?"

"Yes…looks like I am."

He smiled. "I'd love to."

Chapter Seven

Chloe knocked on Gage's door, her heart hammering in her chest. She ran her palms down her simple blue dress and waited. Usually, Gage had stayed in a hotel for the times he'd come to town previously, but that was a weekend at a time. This time he'd rented a studio apartment overlooking the water.

She was on a date. Again. And this time, it'd been *her* idea. But he'd been way too thoughtful—romantic even—for her to let him walk away with nothing. And now she had to figure out how to get through tonight with her panties intact.

Gage opened the door, and her breath caught. Even in a simple white button-up with rolled-up sleeves, dark jeans and barefoot, he was stunning.

She frowned at his feet. "Are you ready?"

He opened his door wide and spread an arm to invite her in. "I'm ready for our date, but I thought the location could be here tonight."

She bit the inside of her cheek. "So we're going to be alone in your house for our date?"

A few days ago, she'd have killed to be alone with him in his house. But that had been when she thought alone in Gage's house meant no clothes and lots of sex. Now it meant more. Now it meant acknowledging that she felt the things for him that she'd promised never to feel.

He nodded. "Yep. And you look beautiful."

She stayed near the front door as he closed it behind her. "Well, per your conditions of romance before sex, I brought my chastity belt."

"God, when you talk all sweet like that, I can't help my heart from fluttering," he teased.

He stepped closer. Between the staying at his place thing and the raw intensity in his gaze, it almost seemed like maybe he was caving after all. Maybe she wouldn't have to actually spill personal details and they could just get down to what they did best.

He leaned in and said right against her forehead, "I was hoping you'd wear something special for me tonight."

Hell yeah she would. This was looking to be more her speed than she hoped. Chloe smiled and nodded, so he took her hand and led her into the open kitchen. The island in the middle was crowded with ingredients and supplies. Gage picked up a lump of fabric and handed it to her.

She held it out in front of her. "You've got to be kidding. You want me to wear an apron?"

She glanced around—was this some kind of prank? All she saw was the simple studio, hardwood floors, the bed in the corner, and not another soul in the room to explain whatever the hell Gage was thinking.

"So let me get this straight," she said. "You wanted a date, I gave you one. Then *I* asked *you* on one. Now you lure me to your place and have me cook for you? You realize I'm horrible at cooking."

He picked up a second apron, fastened it around his waist,

and walked behind the island. "No, I think you're impatient." He winked. "And I want to help you cook."

"I run my own restaurant. I can manage just fine."

He raised an eyebrow. "Who do you think you're talking to?"

Damn. Busted. "What kind of *help* do you mean?"

"We'll do it together. We can make a simple white sauce, pasta, and veggies."

"Why?"

"Because cooking seems important to you."

Those six words hit her chest hard and took root. He was doing it again. Paying attention to what she'd said, to her actions and desires. He was breaking through her walls— what was she supposed to do? The feelings he awakened in her were…complicated.

But she did want to learn something simple. Anything. Then maybe she wouldn't feel like such a failure taking over her mother's legacy. She also realized that Gage hadn't said they'd make crab cakes. He'd picked something else they could make together. Which was thoughtful, because she wasn't ready to fail in front of him or address some of the heartache that came with her mother's memory.

But what she was ready for, and what her emotions were doing, were two different things. While part of her really didn't want to go into anything painful about her mother, her past, or her mother's past…the other part of her really did want to talk to Gage. Because she knew he'd be kind to her and listen.

Yeah…the forest was getting thick and Chloe was getting lost in the density of…emotions. Which was the exact opposite of the casual stance she was trying so hard to take.

What had Gage told her once? Assess the situation first? Yes, that was it exactly. Assess the situation. Keep her footing. Then…engage. Maybe she could take that step and give a little.

Chloe slipped the apron on and walked around the island beside him. "There's not a lot of ingredients here. You're going to make an entire sauce out of milk, butter, and flour?"

He nodded. "And parmesan and spices, but yeah, basically, that's all it is." He turned the stove on and set the butter in the pan. "Sometimes it's about the process and heat, more than the ingredients." He kissed her gently. So incredibly soft. She leaned in for a second—

And Gage pulled away. He threw her a sly smile as he picked up a mixing bowl, totally at ease with her. Was this how a couple behaved? Did they cook and spend time together?

She wasn't sure, but she kind of liked it. The empty space in her chest didn't hurt as bad tonight—but it'd hurt much more when Gage inevitably left that space gaping. No one stayed. Nothing was forever. Least of all a man with a higher calling.

"You ready to get your hands dirty, sweetheart?" he asked.

She looked at the counter full of ingredients in front of her, then the sexy man who was taking her world to a new level of uncomfortable.

If she had half a brain, she'd pull away now before she got in deeper. Instead, she edged a bit closer. "I think I am."

He put the butter in the saucepan over low heat. Chloe looked in and saw the stick was barely melting. She went to turn up the burner, and Gage stopped her.

"Patience, sweetheart. It'll get there, just give it a chance first."

She folded her lips together and glanced at him. Slow and steady. Just like Gage. Melting butter and low heat that turned her into a puddle. Yep, the comparisons weren't lost on her. Gage wanted them to simmer, she wanted them to ignite and burn up. Granted, simmering still got her hot. Only that level of hot lasted a lot longer than a flash in the pan. Pun totally intended.

"Concentrating awful hard there," he said as he used

a whisk to slowly move the butter stick around in the pan. "Want to tell me what's on your mind?"

Actually, she kind of did. But instead of spilling all the thoughts, worries, and hopes she had, she just stared, letting her brain get the better of her.

"Maybe you're thinking about how much you like my stunning personality?" Gage offered.

That made her smile. "I was thinking about your six pack, but sure…stunning personality," she teased back.

"Well at least you like me for something."

"I really do, you know?" she said seriously. "For a lot of reasons."

All joking aside, she'd let that one fact come out. Gage hadn't missed it, either. His intense eyes hit hers. She'd been honest, told him how she felt, and it was as freeing as it was terrifying.

"I really like you, too."

She nodded and moved to start chopping vegetables. She had to slow this touchy-feely train down before the warm and fuzzy express derailed and left her as the world's biggest train wreck.

"You said something the other day that I'm curious about," Gage said, standing by her to take the second knife and cut a zucchini.

"Oh?" Chloe started on the carrots.

"You said you missed your mom before she died. What did you mean by that?"

She cut down hard on the thick carrot and the snap of the root echoed through the silence.

"I um…" She looked at her hands. Steady. Still. She wasn't nervous like she should be. Because anytime this topic was broached, she shook with unease. But not this time. Not with Gage. He was interested in her. In her feelings. And talking about her mother, talking about her own fears, was something she never did. And right then, she wanted to.

"My dad left when I was younger," she started. She could feel Gage's eyes on her, watching every word fall from her lips as she began to spill out her secrets. "My mother was devastated. He *broke* her. Every day after he left was a struggle for her to live. I know that. But she tried. Put on a happy face for my sake. Was an amazing mother. But she was sad. Not a bummed out sad. This was…" She shook her head, remembering how every day she'd watched the light from her mother's eyes fade more and more. As if every day she'd gotten further and further away from the hope that the man she'd loved would ever come back. He hadn't.

And then her mother's slow death had taken a literal turn. She'd discovered she had cancer. Which deteriorated her body while her father's memory deteriorated her soul. On her last breath, she'd still wanted the son of a bitch that'd left them. All it did was make Chloe hate him more. Hate him for how he'd affected her mother until her last hour of life.

And she'd died knowing that.

"I can't imagine how much it must have hurt her to lose him," Gage said.

Chloe closed her eyes to fight back the emotions bubbling up in her. He didn't know how close his words hit home for her. He couldn't. He was just trying to be there for her now, but instead, he was emphasizing her point.

"This sadness ran through her like poison," she said.

He inched closer and rested his big hand on the small of her back. "It sounds like she was a brave woman."

That made Chloe drop her knife to the counter and look at him in surprise. "What do you mean?"

He shrugged and pulled her closer. "It's brave to hold on to something, even when it hurts. It's brave to acknowledge your feelings. She was sad, but she owned it. And she was still a good mother to you. She lived a full life. In part because she let herself love someone, even if that meant letting herself lose them."

Chloe's lips parted. She'd never thought of it that way. But Gage didn't understand. He didn't get it. How could he? He had no ties. He came and went as he pleased.

Her mother had set ties in this town. Set ties in Chloe's father, too. She'd felt all the things that Chloe had seen leech her final years of joy. She'd felt a few years of bliss. And in the end she'd been left with sadness for taking a chance on love. She had to have known the risk, but she'd chosen to do it anyway.

And that was what Chloe held on to. What terrified her.

She looked at Gage, felt his comforting touch against her back, and wondered if she could be brave, too.

Chloe's laugh made Gage's chest do a crazy flip.

"You really got stuck in a tree once?" she asked around a smile, looking at him over the rim of her wineglass.

"Yeah, worse, the rope caught around one of my legs and left me dangling upside down like a damn possum."

She laughed again, and he smiled.

He hadn't been lying when he intimated he knew how much trouble Chloe had in the kitchen, but he knew something she didn't. A good meal was half skill, half heart. And she had enough heart to feed the world—but she was afraid to let anyone get a piece of it.

So he helped her with the half he could. He wasn't the world's best cook himself, but he walked her through the simple pasta recipe he'd perfected over his years as a bachelor. And the hell of it was with her cooking beside him, the dish tasted better than ever.

Now, sitting at the small table, they drank wine and

chatted, and every curve of her lips and flash of those green eyes had him going hard and filled him with warmth. She was gorgeous and guarded, but when those walls came down and he caught a glimpse of the real her, he couldn't turn away. He loved her brazen sass, and this sweeter side? This was something he could get used to.

If she agrees to a long-distance relationship…

And that was the "if" he'd been struggling with for the last week. Whether or not he wanted Chloe wasn't the question—it was the terms he wasn't sure about. Coming back from S&R missions to a woman and a meal like this was all he wanted. The promise alone would let him face the risk of death without the fear of leaving this earth alone.

But would Chloe ever really want him for more than the occasional romp in the bedroom? When he'd started this whole thing, he'd been sure all he needed was for her to agree to one date. Then she'd see—they'd *both* see—how well they fit together.

He couldn't lose hope now. Hesitation could make this whole thing fall apart.

"I'm sure you have a good-intentions-gone-wrong story," he said.

She nodded and sipped her wine. "Yeah. When I was younger, maybe ten, I tried to make my mother dinner for her birthday. But I wasn't allowed to use the stove."

"So naturally you found a way around it," he offered. If Chloe was half as stubborn as a child as she was as an adult, no rules could have kept her from her goal.

"Naturally," she agreed with a sly smile. "We had this little electric grill we used for camping, so I figured I could use that. I brought it into the kitchen, plugged it in, and slapped some deli turkey on it."

"Oh God," he said. He had a pretty good idea of the kind of device she was talking about—it was strictly an outdoor grill.

"Long story short, the turkey burst into flames, the entire top of the grill had fire spitting out, and the smoke alarm went off. My terrified mother ran in and threw baking soda all over it. We were both a mess of white powder and smoke."

Gage laughed. "You weren't hurt though, right?"

"Just my pride."

"I can see that."

"Hey." She tossed a piece of broccoli at him and laughed. "I'm learning."

"You are. Dinner was wonderful."

"Well, thanks for inviting me over and making me cook for you."

"Oh sweetheart, I would never dream of making you do anything. We both know you wanted to."

Her emerald eyes snared his and all seriousness laced her face. "True." She hesitated, glancing at him, then the floor, then him again. She was going to tell him something, and though she was hesitating, he hoped—please God—that she'd go through with it.

She shrugged. "My mother cooked everything well, but crab cakes were her specialty."

He nodded. "You've mentioned this. So tell me how you're going about making them?"

"Not very well at all. You had me thinking, we made a whole meal with a few ingredients…and the crab cakes are the same. Not much goes in them. The whole process should be simple. I saw my mom do it a thousand times. But I still can't get them right."

He nodded. This was the closest to the real Chloe he'd seen yet, and he loved it. Speaking of love… "It sounds cliché, sweetheart, but your mother cooked with love. You cook with… vengeance."

She laughed. "Shut up."

He snickered and sighed. "Maybe try to relax. Stop fighting it. Open your heart to letting the dish be what it needs to be, then let it turn out the way it will."

"You think it's that simple?"

He smiled. "I know it's that simple. That's how it is with anything. You can't force yourself…you can't force *anything* to be something other than what it already is. You let it breathe. You accept it. You love it." He touched her hand. "You do that with these crab cakes, they'll be everything you remember them being."

He let the unspoken words hang between them. They couldn't force their relationship to be anything other than what it was, either. If only she would treat it with the openness he wanted her to use with the crab cakes.

Chloe looked at him. "Maybe," she whispered. Then she stood and walked around to face him. She gently brushed her knee against his. "I had a good time tonight." She ran a fingertip along his jaw. "Thank you."

Just when he thought she'd kiss him…she turned and walked toward the door.

"Chloe, do you want to—"

"I should get going." She opened the front door and glanced back at him. Gage stared as she walked out and quietly shut the door behind her.

They'd had a date. No sex, like he'd wanted. Even better, she'd opened up to him.

So why did he feel like he'd lost the very thing he'd come for? And why did dread lace his veins when he thought of how many more moments he could have with her, in and out of bed, if only she'd let him?

He glanced around the quiet studio. It was empty and cold without Chloe.

For having a night of everything he wanted, he was starting to feel like it was all slipping through his fingertips.

Chapter Eight

Gage paced in his living room and gripped the phone against his ear. He was in Beaufort, training recruits until the next mission came up. He wasn't banned from going out in the field per se, but he had a commitment to finish the training of these recruits first. A commitment that now fell right in the middle of an unexpected mission.

"I can go in the field anytime," he told his boss.

"I know, but everything's been covered. You stay and train, and when you're done, you'll be on the next mission."

Shit. Gage wanted to be out there now. He'd been up last night, listening to the incoming radio transmissions so that he could keep himself from obsessing about Chloe. That was when he'd heard about the group of teenagers missing on the west coast. He'd immediately called his boss, but instead of being sent out himself, he'd been told that the mission didn't need him.

The feds had stepped in with their team, a team Gage was normally a part of. Only he wasn't heading to the west coast. He was in North Carolina, training new recruits instead of rescuing people himself. It wasn't that he didn't trust the other people sent out there instead of him. It was simply that he couldn't live with himself if he discovered those teenagers died out there. He'd never be able to live with himself knowing that if he'd been there, maybe he could have made a difference.

His chest buzzed with the need to help. To run. To roam.

Yeah, some of this frustration came from wanting to be a part of this big mission. And some of it came from Chloe. She'd opened up even more to him, and then she'd walked away. Which made him happy and uneasy at the same time. The woman was tricky, but he thought she was warming up to the idea of finally exploring the romantic side of their relationship. Or she was setting him up to knock him on his ass when she walked away for good.

He mumbled a curse, unable to really think of that, because the possibility stung his chest. Maybe getting out and getting some clarity would be a good thing? Yeah, like going on a fucking mission. If only he could convince his boss.

"The people in training here are doing well and are pretty set," Gage said. "I can leave early if you need."

His boss was quick to answer. "No, stay there, get those NC recruits all trained."

Gage bit his lip. "I can do more. Let me help."

"You know as well as I do it's only a matter of time until someone needs your help," his boss said. "But the training you've done with these guys has shown me you could help a hell of a lot more people if you didn't run off to do so many of the rescues yourself."

Gage's heart punched his chest. "What the hell is that supposed to mean? You think I'm not the right man to rescue those people?"

"Calm down. You're one of the best we have, which is why a lot of higher-ups, including myself, are anxious to put you in a permanent training position."

Gage's stomach sank. "What?"

"The North Carolina branch could use a man like you to oversee the training program."

This wasn't happening. It wasn't enough. It would *never* be enough. He couldn't root himself to Beaufort and never take a mission. He had to make an impact. How would he live with himself if he heard someone died while he'd stayed behind?

Hell no.

"I'm a field man. I don't mind doing the training here and there, but I'm not going to only train."

"There's more than hitting the field," his boss said. "You have the level head to deal with these types of situations and delegate the right teams to the right missions, which is essential to search and rescue."

How had this conversation turned into trying to keep Gage at a glorified desk job? He wasn't trying to diminish the work people like East did, and yes, his boss had a hard job, strategizing the best plan and team for certain jobs. Gage could do that...but at what cost? How would he handle hearing about people they lost on missions and never knowing if he would've been able to save them?

"I'm honored you'd think of me," Gage said. "But that's not what I am. That's not *who* I am. It's not how I'm built."

"Sounds like you've made your decision. Keep doing what you're doing."

"Well, let me know what missions come up. I can be there—"

"I know. But you need to finish training the volunteers," he said and hung up.

Gage gritted his teeth as he resisted the urge to throw the phone. He stared at his suitcase in the corner of the room— he'd never even unpacked.

Who the hell was he to think putting down roots would ever be a good idea?

His plan was crumbling, and if he didn't regroup, it would all fall apart.

"So is this part of your grand plan?" East asked, coming to stand by Gage.

Gage hovered near the bonfire on East's property, glancing across it to look at Chloe. After his earlier failed attempt to get his boss to send him on the rescue mission, he'd gratefully accepted East's offer to join him and his many other friends for a barbeque. If he couldn't be out on a rescue mission, he'd focus on the mission he'd come here to finish. Because truth was, Chloe hadn't reached out to him since their date the other night.

Something in his heart had shifted that night. When he thought about the situation he'd put them both in, he had a hard time breathing. The possibility of leaving was more difficult to swallow than before, but so was staying.

"You're just going to stare her down without saying anything?"

"Maybe," Gage said. He had a plan. But after their date the other night, he was feeling less at ease about it. What had felt like a win-win was getting more complicated. He'd been so focused on what it meant to be with Chloe that he'd pushed one big issue to the back burner.

Staying.

And thanks to his boss, he now had the word at the forefront of his mind.

The word made his damn mind do somersaults. He wanted a lot of things, but Chloe was at the top of the list. After having an amazing evening with her, then another, he wanted to spend all his free time with her. So why did the idea of sticking around feel so heavy?

Maybe because it's becoming more real…

And therein lay the snag she'd been warning him about from the beginning. It had nothing to do with wanting her — just the logistics of keeping her. They'd spent every encounter up until the other night in a fantasy world. It'd always been temporary, but now he didn't have to leave. This time, whether he stayed or went was a choice and it was daunting as hell.

He drank his beer. The night was beautiful — clouds hung low, and the smell of impending summer rain was in the air. But East was right. While Gage was pretending to look at the bonfire, he was really staring at Chloe standing across from it.

"Speaking of staring," Gage said, changing the subject. "The cute girl in glasses keeps glaring at you. What's going on there?"

East laughed. "Ah, sweet Natalie. She's hated me since we were kids."

Come to think of it, everyone there knew each other. Likely had for a long time. For a while, Chloe had been one of the few people Gage hadn't been familiar with. And then that had changed. She'd gone from the intimate stranger he had casual sex with and instead had become…

That was the hell of it all. He had no idea what she had turned into. Or what she would become. What *they* would become. All this time, he'd assumed that if she just gave them a chance, they'd automatically see how well they fit together.

But his brilliant blackmail plan was biting him in the ass, because now he was messing with something he might not be able to get out of: a commitment to staying.

I can commit to a woman, but not a place…

That little gem of truth his buddy had laid down on him earlier was now pulsing harder than ever in his brain.

"Word around is the head of the Carolina Search and

Rescue core retired and they're looking to replace him. Rumor is they even offered this job to a specific person and still haven't heard if said person is going to take this job." East eyed Gage. "Hmmm, I wonder what this *mysterious person* will choose…" He tapped his beer and grinned at Gage.

Gage nearly knocked his friend flat on his ass. "So it was *you* who told the boss it should be me in the training position."

East shrugged. "All I said was we should look for the right person."

"This *person* is probably thinking training instead of searching is bullshit."

"It's a job, dude," East said. "A good one. One you enjoy and you're good at. This isn't a hard choice."

"I enjoy my job *now*. This new gig would be less fieldwork and more overseeing, scheduling, planning, and training."

"Which you're good at since you're a tight-ass who always has a plan."

Gage hit his friend with a hard look, and East held up his hands. "Don't get your panties in a wad. I'm just telling you what I see. But I'd hate to offend your delicate feelers and get on your shit list."

"My shit list is color-coded, asshole. And yeah, you're officially on it now."

East laughed. "Of course it is. Well then, in the spirit of friendly advice, maybe put down the spreadsheet and think about what you really want."

"That's what I've been doing." Gage glanced back at Chloe. But it wasn't as simple as what he wanted, because what he wanted conflicted with how he operated. He was a man on the move all the time.

"Any epiphanies?" East asked.

Gage shook his head. "No." What he wanted hadn't changed, but the way to go about it had. Maybe he needed more time. Staying wasn't an option, but coming back regularly was. Keeping with his current routine was best. He got to come into town and be with Chloe. Hopefully more often, assuming he could convince her dating wasn't so bad.

Either way, he could have Chloe, right?

For the first time, he wasn't sure. This wasn't a weekend in and out. This was more time, which was creating more of an attachment. It'd be so much more difficult to leave now, and yet staying terrified him.

"There's a lot I have to consider," Gage said. "I don't have enough data yet."

East shook his head. "So you're going to continue pursuing Chloe until you gather your data?"

"You say that like it's a bad thing. I like her, so either way—"

"Either way, this could end badly," East said.

"Since when do you know about pursuing relationships?"

"I openly admit I know nothing about relationships, and I'm good with that. But I know a lot about the pursuit. And trust me when I say you're doing it wrong."

Gage sighed. He wasn't doing it wrong; he was being smart. Diligent. He was trying not to think with his dick, otherwise he wouldn't have been blackmailing Chloe the way he was. So what the hell was East talking about?

"You going to tell her about the possibility of staying?" he asked.

"No, because I'm not going to be a trainer. And I don't want to put that kind of pressure on Chloe."

She already hated the notion of commitment longer than a weekend. If Gage moved here full time? He wasn't prepared to see the terror on her face with that admission. No, he'd stick to his mission of getting her into a long-distance relationship. If she didn't tell him to fuck off first...

And we're back at square one.

"Still something to think about," East said.

He drank and looked at Chloe again. He could get a grip. Find a balance and deal with this situation. If he used this time wisely, really slaked his need for her, at the end of this stay it'd be easier to leave for both of them. Hopefully she'd want him to come back. Hopefully she'd wait for him.

Or maybe he was insane.

"More data," Gage repeated. It was all he could cling to. Getting lost in Chloe for a week or two was a hell of a good way to spend his time—and it'd clear things up in the process. At the end of his time here, he'd have a good idea of what Chloe wanted...and whether he could provide it.

Or maybe he'd hit the road for the next mission, and this time, she wouldn't wait for him to come back.

And if that was the case, could he really blame her? He wanted Chloe to want and miss him, but he couldn't stay. Which made him a special kind of asshole.

No...you've been honest. Haven't over-committed to anything.

He wanted her for the time he was there to see where it went. But now the follow-through was getting slippery. He'd gotten a glimpse of the real Chloe the other night. And yet...

"Look, I don't know what your deal is, but staying isn't so bad," East said. "Having some roots and a nice girl to come home to sounds great to me."

Gage snorted. "Says the town playboy."

"Why do you think I stay? There're a lot of pretty women around these parts." He winked. But Gage didn't miss the way East shot a glance to the chatting brunette in glasses across the bonfire.

Despite his best intentions, Gage knew one thing still to be true: he was capable of committing to a woman, but not a place. But between their sexy mock search and rescue and her inviting him to her restaurant, he had to hope he was gaining ground.

Chloe finally tossed him a smile, then quickly glanced away. So he was in her mind. He was in her thoughts. And if the way she'd begun to open up to him was any indication, he was close to being in her heart.

That was enough to work with.

There had to be a way to have Chloe and freedom.

"Hottie McSearchy keeps staring at you," Natalie said to Chloe.

Michelle leaned into the huddle they had going on and peered over the fire. "Which one is he?"

"He's the one in the black T-shirt with the black hair and black eyes," Natalie said. "Basically, he's the tall, dark and buff one."

"Thanks, Nat," Chloe mumbled and sipped her beer.

East's summer bonfires were casual and frequent, and Chloe hadn't expected to see Gage. But…she was kind of happy to see him. The last couple of days since their date had left her thinking about a lot of things she shouldn't. She was trying to focus on preparing for the anniversary event, yet her mind always drifted back to Gage.

How he made her feel safe whenever he held her. How he mastered the art of being intense and casual all at the same time. How he made her think…made her *want*. Yeah, Gage made her want a whole hell of a lot. Like more. Not that she'd ever really admit that to him, or herself even.

"And who is that?" Michelle pointed at the guy next to him.

"Easton Ambrose," Natalie said with a huff. "He's annoying."

"And handsome," Michelle said.

Natalie's head snapped up, almost like she cared.

Interesting. It was no secret East had a reputation with the ladies, and Natalie had…her cupcakes.

"Well now that we've addressed everyone's staring problem…" Chloe nudged Natalie's shoulder.

"Hey, as far as I can tell, the guy drooling at you from the other side of that inferno is the one with the problem," Natalie said.

Yeah, Chloe was aware of that problem, because she was having some herself. Like thinking too much about him. Which needed to stop. Though the other night had been more real than any she'd ever spent with another man, and her dress had stayed on the whole time. Their date hadn't been a fantasy. It'd been…normal. Like a relationship. And she'd actually liked his company.

She shook her head and tried to get her thoughts clear.

Keep it fantasy, not reality.

"Oh no…" Michelle said softly as a big fat raindrop beaded Chloe's hair.

There was little more warning than that. The clouds unleashed gallons over all of them and beat down on the fire, sending everyone scattering to their cars or inside East's house.

"I was going to take off anyway," Natalie said loudly, unconcerned about the rain.

Michelle ran up to them, the poor girl's perfect hair now a soggy mess. "Can I get a ride with you?" Michelle asked, and Natalie nodded. Chloe tossed her empty beer bottle onto the extinguished fire and headed for the car.

"Not afraid of the rain?" Gage asked from behind her. He held up his jacket like an umbrella and covered her head with it.

"It's water. Nothing scary," she said.

Water she wasn't worried about, but Gage getting closer? Much more nerve-wracking. He was the one man who made her heart shake in her chest, and the closer he came, the less she could deny how she felt about him. And that terrified her.

She looked into his intensely dark eyes. With the orange glow of the fire gone and the clouds muting the light of the moon and stars, Gage's gaze slid over her skin like a touch she wanted to get lost in.

She knew better, but he was her drug, and with him in front of her, she couldn't say no.

She took a step forward, stood on her toes to kiss him—

"Ah!"—and fell right on her ass in the mud. "Oh, God."

Gage smiled and bent to help her up. Mortification surged through her like hot water. This was nowhere near a fantasy. This was real and embarrassing, nothing sexy about it.

She moved to run away, but Gage caught her arm. "I thought you weren't afraid."

Right then, with his hand on her skin and his gaze searching hers, fear buzzed in her chest. But it wasn't the rain, or even him setting it off—it was something deeper, something she'd been denying for weeks.

She couldn't do this. She couldn't stay. It was getting too real.

"I'm not. I'm fine," she fibbed and hustled away. Gage caught up with her near the tree line before she reached her car. Everyone had left. A few people were inside East's house. Gage closed in, the splattering sound of his boots tromping through the mud made her skin buzz. His entire presence was engulfing her.

He pressed against her. "When are you going to stop running?"

"When are you going to stop chasing?"

He stared at her for a long moment, uncertainty in his normally confident gaze.

"What if I said I wanted to keep chasing you for as long as I was in town?"

"I'd say you're crazy."

He dropped his coat, and the rain pelted them both. Even beneath the tree and in the darkness, she felt him. Smelled him. Wanted him.

"You come in and out of town," Chloe said. "Anything longer than a weekend complicates things. Don't you see that?"

He nodded, and Chloe arched an eyebrow. He was agreeing with her?

"What if complication was a consideration?" he asked.

"It doesn't work that way, Gage." She wiped her brow and moved her hair off her face as rain streaked down from the top of her head to her neck. "You come in for a weekend, we have a good time, and you leave. That's worked well for us, but anything longer comes with…"

"Strings?"

Truth was, she was more attached to him than ever—and it terrified her. The more she felt for him, the more power he had over her emotions. Her heart.

Distance had provided an excuse before, but now he was standing in front of her, in her town for a few weeks, and she wanted to touch him all the time. She could think of little else—which was a problem. She was dangerously close to handing her heart over to a man for him to do as much or as little with it as he wanted.

And then, after everything, he would leave.

"We have great sex," she hedged.

Gage frowned. "Can you look at me right now and say this is still just sex to you?"

She pursed her lips. No, this was absolutely more than sex, but she couldn't say that.

"This is why I don't date," she whispered.

He ran his fingers over her cheekbone. "It's only been a week."

"It's more than that." It was the past two years. It was the way he looked at her, the way he tapped into every fantasy she had, the way he gave a damn. The way he made her cave.

She'd given in to him, and deep down, a raw part of her heart was already at his mercy. But there was no way she'd admit it.

No, she needed to get out of this wet, increasingly real moment. Now.

But when she tried to pull away, he grabbed her arm and stopped her.

"Don't look at me," she said.

He cupped her chin and lifted her face. "Why?"

"I have makeup everywhere and I'm all muddy and—"

"And you're still gorgeous." He took her hand. "Stop running, Chloe. Let go so we can fall together."

She didn't know exactly what he meant, but he took her several yards away from the house and down a small hill as the rain pounded on their shoulders. When they reached the crest, he tugged her with him and slid down the muddy hill.

She screamed and laughed, and Gage was right there with her.

He rolled over to face her, covered in mud and grinning ear to ear. "See, dirty isn't so bad."

"Maybe you're right." She scooped up a big handful of mud and slapped it on his cheek.

"Oh, you're going to pay for that, sweetheart." He smeared mud on her thigh.

"Oh, it's on now," she said and leaped on him.

He hit his back on a thick patch of grass. She straddled him, but instead of searching for mud, she gripped his shirt and kissed him hard. The thick scent of rain and grass surrounded them. Her clothes were plastered to her body, and she wanted to peel them off and feel his skin.

The heat was too much to bear. It burned up every ounce

of willpower she had. She wanted—*needed*—to feel him closer. Experience him again, because he was better than any roller coaster and gave her an incomparable adrenaline rush.

Gage caught on real quick and kissed her back. There in the sopping grass, she tugged on his shirt, and he hiked up her skirt. His hands slapped against her ass and flecks of water tickled her skin as he ground her body against his.

"Is this still reality or fantasy?" He pulled her bottom lip into his mouth.

"Both," she murmured. She floated somewhere between the ground and sky, between emotions and lust. She couldn't stop, and she didn't want to—she needed him.

He ran his hands from her thighs, up her back, and then cupped her neck. He tilted her head and kissed her hard. Plunged deep to taste her, worked her lips with his powerful tongue. He relaxed further into the grass, grinding against her and sampling every inch of her mouth. His every muscle was straining and taut beneath her. The ridge of his hard cock pulsed between her legs while his biceps and abs flexed and cut out of his skin.

He was fighting something within himself. She sensed it. Felt it. As if content with having her stay right there with him, while also fighting the urge to push. But push for what? Push her for more? Or push her away?

She slowed her kiss, ready to ask if what she was reading from his body was right, but he didn't let her get a fraction from his mouth before he yanked her back.

"Don't move away from me. Not tonight."

"What's happening, Gage?" she asked. Because something was happening. With him. With her heart. With their relationship.

"I'll have to leave at some point."

"I know," she whispered against his mouth. He had missions to go on. But he held her like maybe he'd come back.

Like he'd just travel for work for a few days and that was it. Not the end of the world surely. Or maybe she was reading into his hold on her. Maybe she wanted him to stay more than she'd realized.

"You're here now," she offered.

"Yes, and this is where I want to be."

That was all she needed to hear. Gage wanted to be here. With her. That was something, right?

Chloe nodded and found his mouth with hers once more. She wasted no time unfastening his pants. Keeping his hot kiss on her, he reached between their bodies, grabbed a condom from his pocket, and slid it on. She couldn't wait any longer. She was starved for him, and he wanted her, too. Wanted her to stay.

"Gage," she whispered. She moved her panties aside and surged down on him, hard and fast and dirty.

So dirty, and she loved every single second.

"Fuck, baby, yes," he groaned. With one arm wrapped around her middle and fusing her to his body, the other reached up and yanked down the top of her dress. Cool rain pelted her sensitive breasts, hitting her nipples and beading them so hard she moaned.

"Don't you dare stop." He pulled her down even further on top of him until her breasts bobbed above his face. He latched on, sucking the entire peak into his mouth. She gripped the grass on either side of his head and bore down. Rocking back and forth in hard, distinct thrusts, keeping him deep while hitting every internal nerve.

"Stop?" She whipped her hips again. "I'm just getting started."

He grinned and bit her nipple gently. She gasped—the sting of his teeth and the rain pelting her skin lit her up like a bolt of lightning hitting the ocean.

Her knees dug into the soft wet ground as she moved

over him. She shifted her hips to take him deeper. Everything fell away when she ground down so hard the tiny bundle of nerves pressed against his pelvis and his cock rubbed that perfect spot inside.

"Oh God." She whipped her hips again. "Oh yes, right there."

"Making yourself come on me already, sweetheart?" He gave a final kiss to her breasts, then threaded his hand in the back of her hair, bringing her face to face until the tips of their noses touched. "Do it. Use me to make yourself come. Let me feel it."

She was helpless not to. He was giving her power to take him. Use him. Feel him. And she would. Because reality or fantasy, she had him right now. All his strength and power was under her, and she was clinging to it. To him.

Her inner walls tightened, her stomach fluttered and tensed as thick lava climbed her spine...

"Thatta girl. I feel you. You're right there. So fuckin' sexy, sweetheart."

His dark rasp was all it took to kick her release over the edge. Her body cracked and popped with an orgasm so intense it felt like she'd been shot from a cannon. Over and over she gripped him, seeking more but on the brink of too much.

This right here, as he looked into her eyes and they moved in sync, this was more real than ever before. This was the connection she'd been running from for so long—and now that she'd had a taste, would anything less be enough?

He growled her name and lifted her up, spinning her and pushing her back against the ground. Blades of grass scratched her skin while Gage's hot flesh pressed against her front. His massive body mostly shielded her from the downpour, and his dark eyes practically glowed in the night, like a predator. Like a man on the brink of devouring her.

"Don't you dare stop," she said, repeating his command to her. She bit his ear as she threw her hips up to take his length in and out of her. "This is what I've wanted." She grabbed his ass, digging her nails in, and he groaned to the sky.

"You make it hurt," he said, so much pleasure lining his voice.

"So do you."

"Do you like it as much as I do?" He thrust hard back inside her.

"Yes…maybe more."

"Impossible," he whispered into her hair, then kissed her. His wet chin scraped against hers and the prickle of him taking up every inch of her body was consuming.

In and out he took her, each surge inside more powerful than the last. He drove his arms beneath her shoulders and wrapped her in a hug, clutching tight as he worked faster and faster.

She gasped his name as another release spired through her body like pop rocks in soda. He held her so tight that she thought he might never let her go.

"Chloe…there's got to be a way." He groaned as his body stiffened, and he gripped her even tighter as his release flooded him. He shuddered against her.

There's got to be a way?

What was he getting at? Was he saying there must be a way for them to be together? To make this work? To date?

She wasn't sure, but as his strong chest rose over her, she knew no matter what was possible, reality always won out.

As they caught their breath, she opened her eyes to rain crashing down on them. This wasn't a fantasy. This was real. And she had no idea how to get out.

G age unlocked his front door and ushered Chloe inside. They were both caked with mud. He'd never felt more alive than when he was inside her, surrounded by nothing but nature and her skin. His back still hummed from where the rain had hit him as he drove in and out of her.

Elemental, primal, wild.

Everything he experienced with her tapped into the next level of need. Any time, any place, he wanted her—and he didn't want to give her up.

His plan was becoming heavier by the second. His team was out there without him when he ought to be out there helping them find those people—how was he supposed to give that up?

Gage shook his head—he'd deal with it later. Every moment spent with Chloe pulled him deeper and deeper into a situation he wasn't sure how to tackle—but he couldn't stop. Not now. Not when he'd already come this far.

He needed to show her they could work while he was here. That even when he left, they could still have a relationship of sorts when he was away. He'd visit more often, stay for longer periods of time. Surely he could make that good enough and have it both ways…

"Come here." He walked her into the bathroom, turned on the shower, and faced Chloe. "I really want to say something about you being such a dirty girl…" He smiled and tugged on her sodden dress. Mud streaked all over her legs and in her hair. She looked like a wild Amazonian goddess.

"If you did, I'd counter with you're the one who makes me dirty," she said lowly.

"Is it bad that I like that?"

She shook her head. "No, I like it, too."

He took off his shirt, then his jeans, and when they were both naked, he led her under the spray of the water. He lathered up soap in his hands and washed her neck. His thumbs slid along her jaw, massaging and cleaning away the mud.

It was incredible how she responded to him. They were naked, yet this wasn't sexual. It was almost...nurturing. He was happy to just touch her. Revel in her beauty and wash her. Keep her close.

"So, we both want to be dirty together," he started. "Why don't we?"

She peeked open an eye. "What?"

"Give in to me," he whispered.

"I gave you your date. And romance."

"I know. But I want more." His hands roamed from her chest to her arms, spreading the bubbles. "I don't know when I'll be called out on the next mission, but I want you to spend however long I have left here with me. We can—"

"Pretend there's more between us than there actually is?" she snapped.

"That's where you and I differ. I *know* there's more between us."

"There can't be," she said. "You know how bad that'd be."

"So you want to keep doing what we're doing without ever exploring more?"

Her wide eyes searched his face. She wanted to say something—it was on those pretty lips, but she held it back and glanced away. He grabbed the soap and placed his lathered hands on her chest.

"Tell me the truth," he said. "What is it you want? Beyond the sex, beyond a casual and temporary relationship. What do you honestly want?"

Her hands stilled. "I want to be the fantasy...not the reality."

Her words smacked straight to his gut. She'd rather live in suspended bliss with no thought of a deeper connection than risk being real with him. Maybe they were further apart than he'd thought. But behind her perfect skin and sweet face was a hint of fear. Was she afraid of him? Afraid of more? Could he convince her this long-distance type of relationship could work?

Before he could ask, her green eyes fastened to his. "What is it *you* want, Gage? Beyond the date, what do you honestly want?"

The truth hit him hard. "I want you to miss me when I'm gone."

Her chest rose on a sharp breath. In a few words and a single admission, the difficulty of their situation blared like fog lights in a storm. Dread gathered in his stomach.

Could they both have what they wanted?

Maybe this was why fantasy was better. Reality could hurt.

They didn't say anything else. Just finished cleaning up while their words and tonight's events settled over them. He wrapped Chloe in a towel and took her to bed.

"I should go," she whispered.

But he tucked her under the covers and climbed in behind her. Because God help him, he couldn't send her away. Not when she was so close.

Would they ever have a shot at anything more than this fantasy? It seemed less and less possible.

He hugged her against him. "Stay here tonight. In my bed. In the fantasy."

She didn't say anything, but she didn't try to leave, either. Her soft, even breathing was all the answer he needed for now. Because at least for tonight, she'd stay. In his arms. In the fantasy. Even though he couldn't get reality out of his mind.

Chapter Nine

Chloe opened her eyes and stretched. The soft covers floated around her like a cloud, surrounding her in warmth, tranquility, and…

Panic.

She was in Gage's bed. The soft light of late morning filtered through the room and warmed her face, but he was nowhere to be seen.

What had happened? She'd had sex with Gage…in the mud, during a rainstorm. He'd taken her to his place, and then they'd showered and gone to bed without having sex again. What had he been thinking? What had *she* been thinking? Showering without sex. Sleeping in the same bed without sex. The only people who did that were people in relationships. The kind of people she'd insisted she and Gage could never be.

She should have left him last night as soon as she saw where this was going. Instead, she'd lain there, her head against his chest, and had fallen asleep.

What had she been thinking? What had he been saying?

Everything in the light of day felt more like a mess than last night, which was an *actual* mess. He wanted to see where things went between them? Like on a serious level? Dating?

She shook her head. No. He'd be gone as soon as the next mission came his way—then everything would go back to normal. He'd get caught back up in saving people, and by the time he came back, he'd have forgotten about changing what was between them into something that couldn't last.

Damn him. Damn him for making her care about him. Damn him for opening her up to the kind of loss she couldn't face. She'd seen how love—and loss—had destroyed her mother. She wouldn't let it destroy her, too. She knew better.

This had to stop. She was already getting too attached to Gage. Usually, he'd be gone by now and she'd never have the chance to think these things, to *feel* for him. Except he'd been here for a few days, and already her heart was opening to him in ways it never should.

She should cut this off now. Tell him to leave her alone, at least for now. Maybe forever.

The front door opened, and Gage walked in carrying a paper bag. He headed her way, set it on the bed, and quickly kissed her lips. She glared at him.

"Well good morning to you too," he said.

"I need to go." She started to roll off the bed, but he stopped her.

"I got you a sandwich." He unwrapped the food from the bag and handed it to her.

She lifted a slice of bread and examined the ingredients. "No bell peppers or mustard?"

"No. I thought you hated those."

"I do," she whispered. He knew her so well—down to how she liked her sandwiches…

He knew *her*.

She shook her head. "I really should go."

"I didn't poison your food," he said sarcastically.

She got up and tugged on her dress, which had dried mud on it, but she didn't care. Her place was only a few blocks away, and if walking down Main Street looking like a slob was what she had to do to get out of there, she would. Because the world was crashing around her and she was losing hold on her safe indifference.

"Tell me what's going on," he said.

She tugged on her shoes.

"Chloe," he snapped. "Tell me what's wrong."

She looked at the ground and shook her head. "I like you so much." She dared a glance at him.

He smiled. "That's the best thing I've ever heard."

"That's just it," she said. "I don't want to like you!"

He staggered back like she'd punched him in the stomach. "Why?"

She felt horrible, but the words were out there, and she couldn't deny them. She tossed her hands in the air. "Because I know myself." And the emotions running within her. Whenever she wanted something, she clung to it. Hard. With teeth and nails—with her entire being. And she'd learned the hard way even with your tightest hold, what you wanted could still be ripped away.

Worse, it could choose to walk away.

She wouldn't go through that. Love stories were a cliché no one could live up to. Better to never love at all than suffer this kind of pain. Even thinking about Gage dying in the field or one day walking away from her—the very thought made her shrivel up inside. If it actually happened, she'd die inside.

But she couldn't come out and say, "The reason I can't be with you is because I want to be with you." It'd never make sense, but it was how she worked. She clung too tightly to what she loved, which was why she couldn't let herself love anything.

No matter how hard she'd tried to be different, it was the truth. Her mother had clung to the stupid notion that her father loved them and would come back someday. She'd clung to fantasies that didn't exist. And now Chloe was on the brink of doing the same to Gage.

And she couldn't do it. Her heart couldn't handle it, and it wasn't fair to him. Even if she dared to believe that he was serious about wanting something more permanent with her, he could still die in the field. She could still lose him regardless of how he felt about her.

What was the other option? Ask him to stop helping people? Ask him to stop rescuing someone in need?

Telling him to stay would go against what he loved to do. She'd never put him in a position to pick her over his job.

"We both knew this was never going to last," she said. It was more a statement for herself than for him, but Gage just sat there, next to the perfect sandwich he'd gotten for her. "Let's just enjoy this for what it is."

He nodded once, his face like stone.

Her eyes stung. The words hurt her as much as she knew they hurt him. But she turned and walked out before she could take them back.

"What do you think it means?" Chloe asked, eyeing the vase of flowers that'd been delivered a few minutes ago.

Natalie came up to the bar and placed a cupcake in front of Chloe. Chocolate on chocolate, her favorite. "Usually, people smile when they look at a big vase of flowers, not glare at it trying to mentally make it burst into flames."

Chloe huffed. "I don't trust it." She hadn't seen Gage since she'd walked out on him the other day, and now there were flowers. What the hell was she supposed to think?

"Did you at least read the card?"

"As a matter of fact, I was just about to."

She swallowed, picked the little card out of the flowers, and read:

I'm sorry I haven't been around much. I've been busy with training.

But I've been thinking of you and will see you soon.

Love, Gage

Chloe scoffed at the little smiley face Gage had drawn at the bottom of the card to go with his words.

"I think it means he likes you," Natalie said, as if it were obvious.

Chloe took a big bite of her cupcake and stared at the flowers. She'd never gotten flowers before, and it left her feeling...giddy.

She shoved the rest of the cupcake in her mouth, crossed her arms, and glared some more. She'd never asked for an explanation why he hadn't called. She *knew* why he hadn't called. She'd walked out on him.

But he'd given a reason anyway. And it was just like him not to come down on her for making a mistake. Instead, he'd put the blame on himself.

He also said he'd see her soon, which probably meant the anniversary event. In the meantime she had to...trust him.

Natalie whistled and raised her eyebrows. "I know you're new to this whole dating thing, but trust me, acts of kindness are a good thing."

She shook her head. "That's just it. He's being kind when I should be the one apologizing."

"Whoa." Natalie held out her hands. "You mean you're admitting you're wrong?"

"No," Chloe said quickly. "I mean it's not a matter of right or wrong. I just...don't want to like him." She meant it.

This need to see him, to want to be around him, this constant wondering what he was doing, it was taking over her mind. She was practically obsessed.

Not good.

"It's a vulnerable place to be. Wanting someone and hoping they want you back."

Natalie glanced away, and a flash of sadness crossed her face. But she blinked a few times then plastered on her trademark sunshine smile. "But Gage clearly wants you back so what are you worried about?"

"Because I know him." Gage's need for change, for adventure... He was a flight risk, and she *knew* better.

She glanced at the flowers again. Maybe he could stay—better, maybe he'd want to. Maybe he really did want more with her, and maybe she could make it work with him.

Maybe...

"I need to focus on getting ready for the event," Chloe said.

"Ah yes, why acknowledge this when you could avoid it instead?" Natalie answered.

"What do you mean?"

"You have a man in front of you, Chloe. He's trying to make this work. And you're shutting it down."

Chloe shook her head. "I have a good reason." By age six, she'd stopped counting how many times her dad had taken off. She'd stopped keeping track of her mother's tears and bouts of depression by age nine. It had come as no surprise that final time her dad left and never came back, or that her mom never stopped waiting for him.

Now, as an adult, there was an emptiness in Chloe that still wouldn't go away. She wasn't worth sticking around for, and she didn't want another reminder. Not with Gage. To love someone and lose them was a special kind of torture.

Not that she was in love with him...

"You may have a good reason, but Gage has nothing to do with those reasons. He's not your dad, but you're making him pay for those mistakes."

Oh crap. Natalie had a point.

"Maybe it's time you try a different tactic. Otherwise you may lose out on something worth keeping."

Chloe closed her eyes. If that didn't seal the fear in her heart, nothing would.

Maybe...

It was terrifying how a single word gave her hope and fear all at once. The last thing she wanted to risk losing was Gage.

"I need to focus on the event," she finally said and walked back to the kitchen. But she didn't make it. She turned around and bolted back to the counter, fishing her cell phone out of her pocket.

"What are you doing?" Natalie asked.

"I have to talk to Gage." She dialed his number and held the ringing phone to her ear. She had to tell him she cared. Had to say...something. Anything. Because for once, she'd try feeling her emotions instead of hiding from them.

"Hey," Gage answered quickly.

"Hi. Listen, I got the flowers and was wondering if maybe—"

"Sorry sweetheart, I can't talk now," he interrupted. She could hear the fumbling of a pack being zipped in the background. "Got called out. Family is missing over by the campsite and cliffs. I'll call you when I can."

Chloe didn't get another word out. The phone clicked as Gage hung up on her.

She stared at the screen, the flashing numbers showing the call had lasted exactly seven seconds.

"What was that about?" Natalie asked.

Chloe swallowed past the icky feeling rising in her throat. "He got called out on a mission." Which was his job.

Something she knew. Something she understood. Something he couldn't help. So why the ick?

"I'm sure he'll call you as soon as he can then," Natalie offered as if replaying Gage's words.

"Yeah," she agreed, but her smile felt forced. She put her phone back in her pocket and did the one thing she should have done a moment ago. Walked into the kitchen and regained focus on the event.

Not Gage.

Chapter Ten

"No more training, boys, this is the real thing." Gage picked up his pack. Everyone had met at the edge of the forty-acre campground on the outskirts of town where thirty minutes ago, a family of three had been reported missing from their campsite on the outskirts of Beaufort. Gage had the volunteers he'd been working with as his backup.

A little girl and her two parents were missing. That was all the information they had. They could be together, separated, hurt… No one knew, and time was precious.

Sure, Gage hadn't been sent on the west coast mission last week, but this family was missing on his turf. And he had the trainees and the full-time team with him.

This was a mission he could do right now. And he would. He'd find this family.

"The girl was right here, playing by the fire pit," the campsite neighbor said, pointing at the long extinguished coals. "When they didn't come back yesterday, I started to worry and called it in. The girl is six. Her name is April. We're sure the parents went out after her and got lost themselves.

My feeling is that if we find the girl, we find the parents."

Gage's chest was tight. He had to find them, and he had to find them fast. They only had another hour of daylight on their side.

With a map in hand, he assigned quadrants to the different groups of search and rescuers, and then he took off on his own to search.

Six-year-old blonde girl wearing a red shirt and jeans.

Forty minutes in, Gage was scouring every inch of terrain he could. His body was already covered in sweat and his muscles ached, but his training kicked in, and he closed himself off to the discomfort. He'd force his body to continue until the mission was complete. A little girl and her parents were out there. Alone. Afraid. Lost. A minute's rest could be all that stood between them and getting out of this alive.

He spotted small footprints in the dirt, and hope rushed through him.

"April!" he called.

She had to be close.

The sun was setting, and he had to find her before it got dark. Had to. Because the second the light faded, the chances of her surviving…

No! He'd find her first.

A soft sniffle and a hoarse cry came from his left, and he took off toward the sound.

The trickle of a creek filtered into his mind, and with it came Chloe's face. Hard to believe only a short time ago she'd been out here with him. The world had seemed hopeful and bright. Now all thoughts of what could but might never be were sinking in hard.

Damn it—he needed to get his mind straight.

Gage's foot hit a pit in the ground—his leg tensed, a muscle spasm, and his knee locked up, taking him down. He hit the ground hard and clamped his knee with both hands, gritting his teeth. He'd fallen so hard he'd knocked his damn kneecap out of alignment. He slowly bent and extended his leg, trying to force the cap back into place.

"Mother fucker!" He knew better. It'd been a rookie mistake bounding toward a sound without checking the surroundings or terrain. He was too busy thinking about losing Chloe, and now he was losing the little girl he was supposed to be looking for.

He needed to get it together. Now.

Using his knife, he made a small cut in his pants so he could reach in and squeeze both sides of his kneecap, angling it just right...*pop!*

Gage hissed, but his knee was back where it should be. Deep breath and a "thank God" later, he was up and walking. Sore and with a limp, but he'd worry about that later.

He called out again. "April? Can you hear me? Say something, honey, so I can find you."

"H-help," a soft voice squeaked out. Gage moved toward the sound, and in twenty paces, he found the small girl with her knees pulled to her chest, crying next to a tree.

Relief enveloped him. "April." He crouched next to her. "My name is Gage. Are you hurt?"

She shook her head. "No. I can't find my mom, but she's looking for me. I heard her earlier, but I couldn't find her."

Gage nodded. April must've run off, and her parents went looking for her and got themselves lost as well. Which meant they could be anywhere and were probably split up.

"Do you remember the last time you heard your mom's voice? Was it recently?"

She shook her head. "It was a long time ago."

And Gage had been yelling and gotten nothing from either parent, which meant they were out of earshot. But he had to get the girl back and checked out.

"I'm going to take you to the doctor, okay?"

Her eyes widened. "But my mommy and daddy!"

"I have a lot of friends looking for them right now. We need to make sure you're okay."

April hesitated, then nodded.

He radioed his team. "Found the girl. Require a medic once we reach the campsite. On the way back now. Status on male and female adults?" He said it lightly so April hopefully wouldn't worry.

His radio rang out with the crew leads.

"Nothing yet."

"Nothing."

Jesus. What good would it be to save the girl if he couldn't save her parents, too? Gage picked her up and stood—his knee screamed with pain. He knelt back down and cursed.

"Don't leave me," April whispered. "Please, don't leave me."

He brushed his hand against her face. "I'm not going anywhere, sweetheart."

G age needed to get April to the hospital, then go back out there to help find the parents.

After a half hour walk back to the main site, darkness had fallen and East was waiting with another medic and ambulance to see to the girl.

He set the girl down, and the medic looked at her while East checked out Gage.

"Jesus, we need to get you to the hospital." East examined his leg and the hole he'd cut in his pants to get to his knee. Which was now settling with a nasty bruise over it.

"It looks worse than it is," Gage said.

East crouched down and lifted his pant leg. "You could have a major tear in your ACL," he said. "Come on, you're going to need X-rays."

"I'm good," Gage insisted. "My damn knee just comes off the track now and again."

"Which is *not normal*," East said bluntly. "So go get it checked out."

"Can't," Gage said. "The parents are still missing."

"And there're teams searching. Including the one you trained yourself. You have to get this looked at. I don't know how you're walking right now."

"No."

"Soon as it's checked out, you can come right back to the search, assuming you can walk. Getting yourself lost and hurt out there isn't helping anyone."

Gage sighed. Truth was, it'd help to get his knee wrapped, because it was starting to hurt like a motherfucker. "One hour, max."

"Let's go, smart-ass, before I cut off your leg just to spite you."

As the adrenaline wore off a few minutes later, the pain hit hard, radiating up and down his leg. East was right—it was a good thing he hadn't gone back out into the woods. Maybe it was worse than he'd thought.

"No, no, no, that son of a bitch, no." Chloe hustled through Beaufort Medical Center, her dress constricting and her hair falling from the fancy updo. People would arrive at the restaurant in an hour for the twentieth anniversary event.

She should have been there. Her restaurant, the town, her mother's memory—they were all depending on her. Instead, she was running down a hospital hallway, her heart beating in her throat with worry.

East had called to tell her Gage had been hurt on a

mission and was in the hospital. Then the call dropped before he could finish, but that information alone was enough to steal the air from her lungs.

He had to be okay. Had to be. She'd kick his ass if he wasn't.

He was all she cared about. And she prayed with every step she took that he was okay.

"Please…please…" She rounded the corner and found his room. Chloe burst through the door and found him sitting on the side of the bed as a doctor wrapped up his knee.

Gage's eyes widened. "Chloe? What are you doing here, sweetheart?"

How dare he act so casual? She glanced at his knee, then at his whole leg. He was okay. He was alive. He was hurt, but alive.

She sighed a breath of relief. "East called me and said I had to get here right away. He said you got hurt, and the call was over before he could tell me how bad, and…I was afraid you were…"

She glanced at his knee again as the doctor finished wrapping it.

Gage frowned. "Doc, can you give us a second alone?"

The doctor looked at them both and must have seen something he didn't want to get in the middle of. "Two minutes. I need to get you a shot of cortisone."

Once the doctor was gone, Chloe couldn't help herself. She grabbed Gage and held him close. "You're okay?"

He held her tightly. "Yes."

But she pushed against his chest and backed away, shaking her head. "I was so worried you were hurt. Or worse. Maybe even…" She couldn't finish the thought.

"I'm fine," he insisted. Part of her wanted him to tell her she was silly. Stupid. He was fine and he was here and he was never going to leave her again. But his eyes were distant, like he didn't see her at all. His mind was elsewhere. "I have to go."

"What?" she asked. "You're hurt. Where are you going?"

"Back out." He stood and snatched his clothes off of a nearby chair.

Chloe couldn't believe her eyes. Was he serious? "You can't go back out."

"Yes I can," he snapped. "There are still two people missing."

She'd never heard his voice so gruff before. "Still? Meaning you found someone already?"

"The little girl. But her parents are still out there." He shoved his bad knee into one of the dirty, ripped pant legs.

The stupid heels digging into her pinky toe and the flowy dress she'd gotten for the occasion felt silly now. She was standing in lace and silk and had never felt more scared in her life.

"Gage. I know you care about me. But you have to take care of yourself, too."

He wasn't listening to her. He tore off the gown and yanked his T-shirt on.

"Gage," she tried again, moving toward him. "You're scaring me. I thought everything was back to normal. Completely. And then I get a call and hear you're..." The truth hit her so hard that she felt it like a smack to the face. "I love you," she whispered.

"What?" He cupped her shoulders and pulled her back enough to look into her eyes.

"I love you," she murmured, fighting back tears. "You have to be okay."

He shook his head and broke eye contact. "I love you, too." He kissed her cheeks, and then he stepped away from her. "But I have to get back out there."

It wasn't enough. Even admitting her feelings for him wasn't enough to convince him to stay—and it was breaking her heart. "You're hurt. Aren't other people looking for the parents?"

"Yes, but that doesn't mean anything. *I* need to be out there."

Her heart sank. Nothing she said, nothing she did mattered—Gage had made up his mind. He would leave. He didn't care about his health, he didn't care about her feelings, he didn't care about anything other than finding that little girl's missing parents and making her family whole. And maybe that made him a hero, but it also made the truth undeniable.

"I can't do this," she said.

He froze in the middle of tugging on his jacket and finally met her eyes. "What do you mean?"

"It means I. Can't. Do. This." He had to go. No, he didn't *have* to—he was *choosing* to. She cared about him. He'd already hurt himself and was still going back out… She didn't know what else could happen.

"You don't have to worry about losing me—"

"—if I let you go now," she finished.

Gage stiffened. "Chloe, you're not making sense. I know you're worried, but this isn't that bad. I get banged up all the time."

"You can barely walk, and you want to go back out and scale cliffs?" She cupped her forehead, reality hitting hard. This was the one thing she'd never wanted to face—Gage getting hurt. He could die. She wouldn't know until well after. What if she couldn't get to him? She'd be stuck there, waiting.

Waiting on him.

Waiting for the next phone call.

Waiting to see if he'd choose to come back to her.

Waiting to see if he survived the next mission.

Waiting.

"I can't." She loved him so much it hurt, and she didn't know what to do. There was no way to make it better. No way to cling to someone who couldn't be held. She was losing a man she never had the right to hold on to in the first place, a man she knew better than to reach for. But he'd tricked her into opening her heart to feeling something more for him, and now her soul was paying the price.

"Chloe," he whispered, and pain sliced through his dark eyes. "We can make this work. My job is dangerous, but it'll get easier to deal with."

"You could have been hurt worse. Died, even."

"This isn't the first time this has happened," he said. "I always come out okay."

Her gaze snapped to his. "What do you mean this isn't the first time?" Her skull felt on the verge of imploding. It seemed so obvious—of course he was putting his life on the line every time he went out there, but she had to ask. "How many times have you come close to dying?"

The muscle in his jaw ticked. "Once."

Her lungs shut down. This was real. He had almost died. "When?"

"Few weeks ago. Before I came to Beaufort."

Her mind went numb and her breath caught in her throat. So recently?

"Is that what motivated you to do—to *want*—all of this?"

He nodded. "But I'm fine," he added.

"Really?" she said loudly. "Because you don't look fine. You look like you're injured and you're trying to go out anyway."

"I know my limits," he growled.

"Clearly," she said sarcastically. He was a hero. He had to go, had to be out there, no matter the risk. And she knew better than to fall for a man like that. He'd always put himself in danger—which made him someone she could never be with.

Flashes of what could have been, might have been,

flickered through her brain, and she fought the urge to retch. He could have died, and she would have never known until he was already gone.

"I love you so much," she said again. Anger heated every word, because reasonable or not, she was pissed he'd shown her how much she loved him. How much she'd *always* loved him. "And that's your fault. *You* made me love you. And now you're offering nothing in return."

"I'm offering you everything I'm able to give."

"Which is what? You leaving? Coming in and out of my life with no guarantee you'll ever come back?"

"I'll come back to you. I'll always come back, you just have to wait for me."

And there it was. She had to sit back and wait while he took her heart and soul with him every time he left.

She had to get away from him. She couldn't think. Couldn't breathe.

"Chloe, I have to get back out there now. That little girl needs me to find her parents." He yanked on his boots. "Just wait for me. Please. We'll talk about this later."

No. She was done waiting. She should have been done with this long ago. Maybe then she could have saved herself the heartache she'd always been afraid of.

"I can't wait for you," she whispered. "I'm sorry, but I can't. It's not your fault—this is who you are. Go find those parents."

Gage called her name as she turned and ran out of the hospital, but she didn't look back.

Chapter Eleven

G age wanted to chase after her, but Chloe knew him better than he knew himself. The girl's parents were missing, and he had to go out there to make sure the family was reunited.

His chest was sore, as if Chloe had snatched his heart from between his ribs and run off with it. But he had to focus. Had to get back out there. It was his single objective.

Footsteps and the loud ruckus of conversation drifted into the room. Gage recognized some of the voices from his rescue team just before East stepped into the room.

"Hey."

"Not now," Gage growled.

"Whoa, easy tiger. I was coming to tell you the good news. The parents were found. Thankfully they stuck together and seem to be in good shape."

Gage blinked. The parents were found? The family was okay? And they'd finished the job without him? "What?" His mind and body slowed for the first time in hours. "Who found them?"

East smiled. "The new recruits you trained. They were like carbon copies of you. They moved and examined the area exactly like you taught them. I swear, it was like watching you out there."

Gage was half stunned and happy. The guys stuck to their training and acted on his behalf the way he'd taught them. *He* had done this.

"It's a good fuckin' day, man," East said. "Everyone survived with nothing more than a few scratches."

The adrenaline that'd kept Gage functioning drained from his limbs like an emptying whirlpool. They were okay.

Relief settled in his bones as clarity hit him like a punch to the stomach. Chloe had left him. She'd told him she'd loved him, and then she'd walked away.

He clutched his throbbing knee but nothing compared to the fear, the relief, the instant flood of countering emotions. Was this how she'd felt when she'd come to the hospital and seen him?

He couldn't remember really seeing her or hearing what she'd said. He'd been too busy trying to leave.

"Christ," he muttered. "The event."

The restaurant anniversary she'd been working hard on was tonight, and she'd left it to come to him because she was worried.

And I dismissed her.

"You okay?" East asked. "You look like you could use a beer."

Actually, he could. Maybe taking a breather to figure out how to tackle the situation with Chloe was best. He also needed a minute to sort through what he was going to say. Because his world had been crumbling around him, but he was only realizing it now.

He could try to make this work with Chloe. Surely, he could make this work.

She loves me…

The word rolled in his mind, over and over. She loved him, which made him damn lucky. But she hated that she loved him, and he'd just fucked up royally.

East raised a brow. "So I thought I heard Chloe earlier… I take it you're having lady problems?"

Gage finished lacing his boot. "You could say that. Thanks for telling her to freak her out."

"Hey, there was spotty service and she hung up and rushed over here before I could tell her it was just your leg. Besides, I figured you'd want her to know."

Yeah, he did. But he didn't know she'd react that way. Now he was on the brink of losing her for good. Maybe he already had— No. He wasn't giving up on his mission. It was his most important one yet.

"I'll make it work," Gage said.

"Uh-huh. Because you know what's best, and surely you can waltz in and out and Chloe will fall in line."

Gage glared at him. It'd already been a long day, and now East was pulling this shit again. "What's your problem?"

But East came back with his own glare. "Watching you screw this up from day one is getting annoying. Chloe doesn't do commitment. She doesn't wait around. And you want both from her just on the promise that you can make it work."

"Yes!" Gage slammed his hand on the bed. "I have to make it work, East." He took a deep breath. "I love her."

East's eyes shot wide. "Well, hell. That puts you in a big shit storm then."

"I have to talk to her. She's mad I was going to go back out. Now I'm not since the parents were found, so problem solved."

"Man, you are thick," East said. "If you think that's your problem, you're in bigger trouble than I thought."

"She'll understand I couldn't have sat around and done

nothing while people were in trouble."

"Oh, I agree. She'll understand—in fact, I bet she already *does* understand. But it doesn't change that you fucked up. You put the need to be there for others before taking care of yourself. You know you shouldn't have gone back out. You would've told any of us if we were injured to not go because we'd put everyone at risk going out with an injury. You've got something way worse than hero syndrome. This is bordering on suicidal. And the worst part is that you've got a woman screaming at you with a reason to wake up and see what you're doing, and you don't give a shit."

Gage scowled. "Yes I do!"

"Then stop putting yourself before her. Fuck, stop putting yourself before *both* of you. If you want to be a couple, you have to stop thinking about what you need. This is about more than *you*. It's about *both* of you now. It has nothing to do with your job. You're showing her she can't trust you to make a smart decision."

East's words hit really fucking deep and Gage almost choked on the realization. He was right. Chloe was terrified of commitment, yet she'd dropped everything that mattered to her to be here for him. And all he'd told her was to wait.

"I really fucked up," Gage said.

East clapped his hands together. "Ding, ding, ding! Now you're getting it."

Only now, Gage had to do something about it.

Chapter Twelve

"**D**amn!" Chloe threw the wooden spoon across the room. She wasn't one for dramatics, but she couldn't take any more. The event was in twenty minutes and she was on her final attempt of crab cakes—and it was more burned than the last batch because she'd left it to run to the hospital only to have her heart broken.

She looked around her restaurant's kitchen. Guests were arriving downstairs and she'd have to welcome them soon. Without crab cakes, success, or Gage. She was alone.

The place was quiet and smelled like burned crab cakes and failure. And the stupid part was that she was still waiting.

Waiting for him to come back.

Waiting for him to make it better.

It hurt just thinking of him, because a part of her had been waiting this whole time.

Was this what it had been like for her mom? She'd always assumed her dad had been a jerk who never deserved her mom's love. But maybe there'd been something more there. Gage was the man who'd broken down her walls and made her greatest dreams and fears come true.

And I told him I couldn't take this…

Someone knocked on the door, and she bit back the sob. She ran to the door and opened it, unable to snuff out the spark of hope that it might be Gage.

It wasn't. Why would it be? He was gone. She'd made sure of that.

"Hey," Natalie said.

"Hi," Chloe whispered back.

"Everything okay?"

"Nope," she answered honestly. "I still can't make these right."

Natalie pulled her into a hug. "You know, the food is covered and everything is all ready to go. The chef nailed all of your mom's other appetizers, and the new menu items are set. If you don't have the crab cakes, no one will notice."

"That's not the point," she whispered.

"I know."

Natalie was trying to help, but Chloe just felt worse. She wanted to make something, feel that connection again with her mother, but she couldn't. The dish had beaten her. The reality was Chloe didn't have anything in common with her mother other than getting too attached to people who didn't want her back.

"This was going to be my one thing," she said against Natalie's shoulder.

"I know."

Chloe shook her head, wiped her eyes, and stepped back. "I'm going to go down there. Everyone is waiting."

She also needed a break from thinking. And failing. And reality.

"I just need a sec to freshen my makeup."

"Okay," Natalie whispered. "I'll be right down there with you if you need me."

She nodded and shut the door behind her friend. Everything was geared up to go without a problem. Except Chloe was still alone and had accomplished nothing.

Chapter Thirteen

G age went through the back door of the restaurant and snuck around to the kitchen. He'd technically committed robbery tonight. Though he was calling it "borrowing a set of clean scrubs that were left out at the hospital." But he'd been dirty and his pants were muddy and ripped, and he couldn't show up to Chloe's restaurant like that. He also couldn't spare much time. So blue scrubs it was! He didn't exactly look the part of "the good doctor," but at least he was clean.

He'd come as quickly as he could. Tonight was important to Chloe. Not only would he be here, he'd set right what he should have two weeks ago.

He hoped he wasn't too late since he'd made a stop on the way, but he needed to do something big if he wanted to make up for confirming every one of Chloe's worst fears. Better to be late and get it right than on time and ruin it forever.

Everyone looked to be having a good time and chatting. Technically the place had been open for the event for the past hour, so maybe fashionably late would be okay. Point was, he'd made it. And the stop beforehand would be worth it…

he hoped.

He stayed in the shadows between the bar and kitchen. Everyone was on the main floor, and that's when he spotted her.

Chloe.

She was beautiful. Her dress, hair, face—she was the loveliest woman he'd ever seen. She spoke with everyone, but her smile didn't reach her eyes. In fact, her gaze looked a little glossy.

And it was his fault.

She moved through the crowd so gracefully it made his heart jump, but she didn't see him. Not yet.

Didn't matter. She was his—always had been. And he had to make this work.

Finally, she headed toward the kitchen…

"Sweetheart," he said as soon as she stepped inside.

Chloe jumped. "What are you doing here?"

He slid the small covered dish he'd brought toward her. "This is for you."

She frowned at the dish and shook her head. "Are you okay?" She covered her mouth. "Is the family okay? Did you find her parents?"

"The parents are fine. They're all together again."

She nodded. "So you did your job."

"Actually, I didn't go back out. The team I trained found the parents."

He watched her chest rise and fall on a heavy breath. She cared about him. Worried about him. And he'd made her worry more.

She frowned and her eyes ran the length of him. "Um, Gage…what are you wearing?"

He glanced down the front of himself. "Scrubs."

"Uh-huh." She looked him over again.

"What? You're not into the doctor look?"

A small smile broke her lips. "You look like a GI Joe dressed up to play doctor, right after you jump out of a helicopter and meet the A-Team for a rendezvous at headquarters."

Well, that was better than her telling him he looked like a jackass. Because he felt like one.

"I'm sorry," he said. "I would have dressed up. I really am so sorry, and I just needed to get here. I would have been here sooner, but I—"

"Have a job. People to save. I know. I get it. And I'm not mad about it."

"Actually, I was going to say I had to make this…" He slid the dish toward her again, and she opened it.

"Crab cakes?" she asked.

"A few days ago Natalie said you were struggling, so she gave me the recipe. I don't know if they're exactly like your mom's, but maybe they're close?"

Chloe stared into the dish and covered her mouth with her palm. "They look exactly the same. Thank you." That look in her eye softened. "They're raw."

"Well yeah, I put them together, but *you* are going to cook them."

"I can't," she said.

"Yes, you can."

"Gage, don't. I can't do this with you right now. I have people here and—"

"How much time do you have?"

She shrugged. "Twenty minutes maybe."

"That's plenty to cook these. You don't have to forgive me yet, but these need to be made. Let's go."

"I don't know," she whispered. There was pain in her voice, and Gage wanted to make it better. The scary thing was, he didn't know if this would work either. Didn't know if she'd actually forgive him when this was all done. Didn't know where they stood or if they had any kind of future at all.

All he knew how to do was to stick to the mission. But now the mission was more than going out into the field. It was about more than saving strangers. When it came to him and Chloe, it was about saving *them*.

He heated up the skillet in the restaurant's industrial kitchen. For the moment, they were alone. The faint sounds of the bustling people wafted past them.

"Slow burn," he said, putting the oil in the pan. "You just have to maintain the steady heat."

She looked at him, and he saw something sad in her expression. Was this the look she'd described seeing in her mother's eyes? It was soul shattering. And he'd put that look on her face. He had to fix it. Had to try.

"It's ready," he said, gesturing to the pan.

She tentatively reached for one of the crab cakes. He put his hand on top of hers, stilling her for a moment.

"Remember, Chloe. Don't force it. Just love it."

She looked at him, and for a moment he thought she was going to cry, but then she gently set the crab cake in the oil. Her eyes widened as she watched the appetizer slowly brown.

"Flip it," he instructed.

She did.

The golden color was perfect and in a few moments, it was done.

She scooped it out and placed it on a serve tray.

"It looks perfect," she said. She made the next, then the next, while Gage watched her. She was doing it. On her own. The question was, would Chloe want to be on her own in everything from here on out?

Before he could voice that one question, that one fear, Natalie stepped in and said it was time for Chloe's speech.

With the last crab cake finished, Gage couldn't give her a reason to delay going out there.

She sighed. "I have to go."

"This time I'll wait for you," he said. "Just please tell me you're coming back."

She paused, then said, "I have to go."

And then she walked out of the kitchen and toward the podium in the main room.

The event was going great. The grand reopening for the twentieth anniversary had brought in tons of people, and the refinished balcony was a hit. The band was playing smooth jazz on the small stage they'd set up in the corner, and everyone seemed to be having fun.

Except for her.

She'd been ready to live the rest of her days missing him. And then he was here, the last thing she'd expected, and all those feelings came back to the surface. The elation at seeing him and the fear that this would mean losing him all over again.

Her mother's spirit was definitely around, but so was the pain of loss. And when it came to Gage, she only had herself to blame for pushing him away. But she wouldn't repeat that mistake. Not now. Not ever.

She loved him.

He'd come through for her. Helped her accomplish what she wanted to do. Gave her space to be her own person. She had to do the same back for him.

Natalie nudged her shoulder toward the stage. "Good luck." Her friend looked beautiful in her dress. While the event was casual, a lot of people had busted out button-ups and cocktail dresses for the occasion. The twinkly lights were strung high and lit up the whole place with soft yellows and creams.

"I don't know what to say," she admitted.

"Thank everyone for coming and say whatever feels right."

Great, that shouldn't be too tough. Yeah, right.

With a heavy chest, she walked to the small stage. The band slowed the music and eventually stopped when she smiled at them and stepped in front of the mic.

People gathered around, all eyes fused on her.

"Thank you everyone for coming," she said. Her anxiety kicked up a notch as she looked around the room of smiling faces. "My mother would be so happy. She loved this town. Loved all of you."

The words stuck in her throat. She took a deep breath, then continued. "Funny thing about love…it's amazing. And scary as hell."

Everyone laughed, and she felt the urge to tell them how serious she was. She glanced at the French doors near the back and saw him. Gage.

He stepped from the shadows and smiled at her. Looking at her, seeing her, simply being there for her.

Her breath caught, and her heart stalled.

"Love is really scary," she said softer into the mic, keeping her eyes on Gage. "Because love is a risk. You put everything you have into something, like my mother did with this place." She glanced around quickly. "She put her heart and soul into this place because she believed in it. Because she wanted roots and a home. It was a risk, but she took it. She knew if it didn't work that it'd break her heart, but she loved it too much not to take the chance."

She swallowed hard and locked her gaze back on Gage. He slowly moved through the crowd, and those dark eyes of his never left her face.

"This whole time I've been scared," she said. "I was so focused on the fear of the risk, but nothing good in life is easy, especially love. It's what drives us. And I'm going to let go of the wheel and hope I stay on the road. But if I get lost…" She folded her lips, and the sting in her heart rose as she spoke to the one man she'd ever loved. "I have faith I won't be lost for long. Because there's someone who will come find me."

Gage's dark gaze fused to hers. He nodded with that soft, sexy smile.

Everyone clapped, and Chloe blinked. There were tons of people in the room, but all she saw was Gage.

"Thank you all." The band started up again, and everyone began chatting and dancing. Chloe hustled down the stage and made a beeline for the man she'd hoped would come find her.

She didn't stop until she flung herself into his arms.

Chloe clutched him close. "You shocked me."

"I know. I'm so sorry, sweetheart."

"But you came back."

"I told you I would." He cupped her face and kissed her.

"But I pushed you away, too. I'm sorry. I'm so sorry."

"You're going to have to push a lot harder, sweetheart." He ran his nose against hers. "I'm sorry, too. It wasn't fair to make you worry and ask you to wait for me. If you put yourself in danger, I'd tie you down and refuse to let you go."

She raised a brow, kind of liking the sound of that, but Gage was trying to see things from her perspective.

"I understand now," he said. "I want to be with you. Stay with you. I want to be a part of your world—that's all I've wanted this whole time. But I got scared about losing my purpose."

She faced him and looked deep into those dark eyes. He was being honest, and like it or not, she had to return the favor.

"Baby, I know what your purpose is," she said. "And I'm never going to keep you from it. You're here until you get called again because you need to help people. You need to save them."

"That's just it," he said. "I can save people from here."

She swallowed. "What do you mean?"

"East offered me a permanent training position as head of S&R in Beaufort. That little girl's parents? The team I trained saved them. And I can't explain it, but the pride I felt seeing them fulfill the same purpose I've held on to…it showed me what I really need to do. I can save more people by training recruits than I ever could on my own. And maybe, by sticking around, *you* can save *me*, too."

She closed her eyes, unable to hold back a swell of tears. "What about if they need you for some emergency?"

"I'll still go out on calls if there's an emergency, but day-to-day, I'll be right here. Doing my best to be the man who deserves your love."

Her heart was going to explode with joy. She was still crying, but a smile burst onto her face. "Doesn't excuse you being late to my restaurant's anniversary."

He laughed as he reached into his pants pocket. "I deserve that. But I have a good excuse."

"I know, thank you for the crab cakes."

"I don't mean the crab cakes." He pulled a small box from his pocket—

And the world around her paused.

He knelt on his good knee and winced a little.

"Gage, you're going to hurt yourself!" She went down to her knees, too. "What the hell are you doing?"

He smiled. "Well, I'm trying to propose to you, so if you could stand back up, that'd sure help me out a lot."

Her eyes went wide, and he popped the box open, revealing a dazzling diamond ring.

"Will you let me be yours forever?"

If he'd even suggested this kind of commitment when he

first came back to town, she'd have gladly sent him into the mountains and made sure no one ever found him. But now she knew what life was like without him, and the hope that he could be hers now and forever was too good to ever let go.

"Yes!" She grinned and kissed him hard with everything she had. "I love you."

"I love you, sweetheart." He tugged her closer. "And I hope you like the sight of this face, because you're going to be seeing a lot of it. You'll never miss me again. I'm going to be so close to you you'll be sick of me. You'll be begging for me to go on a mission."

"Can't wait." She smiled and held on to the man who owned her heart and her future.

Epilogue

"I must admit these are the best damn crab cakes I've ever had," Gage said. And they were. Better than anything he'd ever made.

Trays of appetizers circulated around the restaurant, and he adjusted his tie and got a little closer to the beautiful blonde standing by the bar in a sexy fitted white dress made of lace and silk.

She flashed him a smile. They were surrounded by people raving about the occasion. All Gage could do was pull up a spot at the corner of the bar and stare down the sexiest woman he'd ever seen.

"Why thank you," she said. "I made them myself."

He raised a brow and drank his beer. "That right? Well you must have many talents."

She shrugged, and the delicate strap of her dress fell down her shoulder. Gage's gaze fixated on it—he wanted nothing more than to rip it off and take her hard. Right there. Right now.

"I have some talents," she said. "But most of them don't

take place in the kitchen."

She was teasing him, and he was game. Leaning in, he whispered, "Well I'd like to see some of these talents."

"Why, sir. I'll have you know you're hitting on a married woman."

Gage smiled and looked her up and down. "Well your husband is a lucky son of a bitch then."

"He's pretty romantic," she admitted.

"And how long have you been married?"

"About an hour."

He nodded. "You know, if you sneak off with me, tell me about some of these talents of yours, I promise to make it worth your while."

She tapped her chin and glanced at the ceiling. He followed her stare—she was looking at the indoor balcony above. "Well, it'd be better to demonstrate than a visual. Although keeping eye contact is key."

His cock stirred as he pictured that eye contact while she was on her knees before him, taking his cock deep into her throat.

"Well, I'm a fair player, sweetheart. All about reciprocation."

"Oh? You have talents too?"

He nodded. "Yes, I do. You lead the way to a quiet corner and I'd be happy to show you."

She eyed him for a moment. Then the ring on his left hand.

"I see you're married, too. What would your wife say about all these naughty things you're alluding to?"

"Oh, she doesn't have patience for me alluding to anything. I have to put up or shut up."

"Sounds like a smart woman."

"She is."

"Well, either that or she just can't keep her hands off you."

"I have to admit, I can't keep my hands off her either."

She turned and walked off without another word. He shot to his feet and followed her. Keeping her lace train in sight, he wound around the back, to the private stairwell—

He grabbed her hand, spun her around, pinned her against the wall, and crashed his mouth down on hers.

She smiled and kissed him back. "We didn't even make it upstairs this time," she breathed as she tugged on his tux.

"I'm surprised we made it out of the public eye." He lifted her dress.

She wrapped her arms around him. This was right where he needed to be. Home, in Chloe's arms. Because she was the fantasy and the reality, and he wanted equal helpings of both.

"We have to make it quick." She fumbled his pants open. "People will notice we're missing, being the bride and groom and all."

"You know how I feel about quickies." He positioned his cock at her core and growled. "No panties? Careful or I may assume you were luring me this whole time, sweetheart."

"I kind of was," she whispered against his mouth.

Which was fine by him. He'd be happy to be lured by her anytime, because she'd always bring him back home.

He thrust inside of her, instantly wrapped up in his own personal fantasy. And he couldn't be happier.

He kissed her neck. "I love you, Chloe."

"I love you, too."

Acknowledgments

Thank you to my editor Stephen "Thunder" Morgan for all your awesome hard work! Thank you Heather, Katie, Curtis, Liz, Debbie, and the entire Entangled Brazen team. Thank you Jill for being an incredible agent. Thank you to my friends and family.

About the Author

National and international bestselling author Joya Ryan is the author of the Shattered series, which includes *Break Me Slowly*, *Possess Me Slowly*, and *Capture Me Slowly*. She has also written the Sweet Torment series, which includes *Breathe You In* and *Only You*. Passionate about both cooking and dancing (despite not being too skilled at the latter), she loves spending time at home. Along with her husband and her two sons, she resides in California.

www.joyaryan.com

Also by Joya Ryan…

CHASING TROUBLE

CHASING TEMPTATION

CHASING DESIRE

CHASING MR. WRONG

RULES OF SEDUCTION